The man in the canvas coa[t] ... way and grabbed several stacks of tobacco, some cigarette papers, and two bottles of whiskey.

"Put this on our bill, old man," the man said with a sneering laugh, and he and his friend headed out the door.

Law asked, "That happen often?"

"All the time," the shopkeeper said, shaking. "Ever since they come to town."

"Can't anyone stop 'em?"

"Who? Town ain't got no marshal. Them ruffians have the run of the town."

Law knew he shouldn't get involved, but he couldn't let this go unchallenged. "Be back directly," he said and went out the door. He saw the men heading up the street.

"Hey, boys!" he shouted. "Hold up." When he got no response, he yelled, "Stop, you two pukes!"

The men halted and turned. "You talkin' to us?"

"You owe the shopkeep some money, punks," Law said evenly.

"He'll put it on our bill," one said. "'Sides, it ain't none of your concern."

"I'm making it my concern, you chicken-livered scut. Now go back there right now and pay up, or . . ."

"Or what?" the other snorted.

The two men laughed. The laughter stopped when Law shoved back the side of his coat and cleared his Peacemaker . . .

TEXAS TRACKER

SHOWDOWN
IN AUSTIN

TOM CALHOUN

JOVE BOOKS, NEW YORK

THE BERKLEY PUBLISHING GROUP
Published by the Penguin Group
Penguin Group (USA) Inc.
375 Hudson Street, New York, New York 10014, USA
Penguin Group (Canada), 10 Alcorn Avenue, Toronto, Ontario M4V 3B2, Canada
(a division of Pearson Penguin Canada Inc.)
Penguin Books Ltd., 80 Strand, London WC2R 0RL, England
Penguin Group Ireland, 25 St. Stephen's Green, Dublin 2, Ireland (a division of Penguin Books Ltd.)
Penguin Group (Australia), 250 Camberwell Road, Camberwell, Victoria 3124, Australia
(a division of Pearson Australia Group Pty. Ltd.)
Penguin Books India Pvt. Ltd., 11 Community Centre, Panchsheel Park, New Delhi—110 017, India
Penguin Group (NZ), Cnr. Airborne and Rosedale Roads, Albany, Auckland 1310, New Zealand
(a division of Pearson New Zealand Ltd.)
Penguin Books (South Africa) (Pty.) Ltd., 24 Sturdee Avenue, Rosebank, Johannesburg 2196,
South Africa

Penguin Books Ltd., Registered Offices: 80 Strand, London WC2R 0RL, England

This is a work of fiction. Names, characters, places, and incidents either are the product of the author's imagination or are used fictitiously, and any resemblance to actual persons, living or dead, business establishments, events, or locales is entirely coincidental.

SHOWDOWN IN AUSTIN

A Jove Book / published by arrangement with the author

PRINTING HISTORY
Jove edition / March 2005

ISBN: 0-515-13898-3

JOVE®
Jove Books are published by The Berkley Publishing Group,
a division of Penguin Group (USA) Inc.,
375 Hudson Street, New York, New York 10014.
Jove is a registered trademark of Penguin Group (USA) Inc.
The "J" design is a trademark belonging to Penguin Group (USA) Inc.

PRINTED IN THE UNITED STATES OF AMERICA

10 9 8 7 6 5 4 3 2 1

CHAPTER 1

JOHN THOMAS LAW tied Toby's reins to a large rattle-bush. "Looks like we'll put an end to this hunt right soon, boy," the broad-shouldered man said, patting the big buckskin on the neck. Law grabbed a couple of strips of jerky and his collapsible telescope from one of the saddlebags, and took his canteen from where it hung on the saddle horn. Giving Toby another pat on the neck—and receiving a soft snicker and shake of the flowing mane in return—Law turned and headed off through the close growth of live oak, hackberry, and black willow trees.

He stopped behind the trunk of a thick live oak and squatted in the tall grass that ran out from the trees and down across the short expanse of open ground to the worn, shabby cabin. Between him and the log house sat a privy under the shade of a spreading huisache tree. Just beyond the house and partly wrapping around the side to Law's left was a rail corral that backed up against Poesta Creek. There were six horses in the corral, though Law knew that there were only three men inside the cabin. He had been following these men for more than two weeks now, and knew exactly how many horses they had and what the hoofprints of those animals looked like.

He extended the telescope and peered through it, checking out the cabin, privy, and area around the house. The cabin was the most plain construction and in need of repair. It was made of logs, probably cut when the land was originally cleared, with much of the mud chinking now gone. A single door in the center of the front, facing Law, was the only opening in the structure; there were no windows. The flatish roof was also made of logs. Beyond the creek and corral were cleared fields, and the creek curled around to Law's left and into the trees.

Law didn't know how long it would take before the men came out and he could take them—one way or another. But he was a patient man when need be. And though he was eager to get this over with, considering how much time he had spent chasing these three men, he would wait them out. Of course, that didn't mean he had to like it.

He snapped the telescope closed and dropped it into a side pocket of his dark frock coat. Then he rose and moved to his right, where he plopped down behind another live oak. He rested his broad back against a boulder, getting as comfortable as he could. Unenthusiastically gnawing on a piece of jerky while he kept an eye on the cabin, he recalled how he had come to be here.

LAW WAS SITTING with a cup of coffee at Mickleson's, which was just down the street from the Manor House in Austin, Texas, the closest thing Law had to a home. He had just finished supper and was trying to interest the waitress in returning to his room with him, when his friend, Texas Ranger Captain Abe Covington, arrived and put a dent in Law's plans.

"Coffee, Abe?" Law asked, as the burly Ranger sat.

"Can't hurt."

Law waved the waitress over and politely asked her to bring Covington an enameled mug. He offered her his most pleasant smile. Depending on what Covington wanted, Law might still be able to see the consummation of his plan. He was rewarded with a saucy grin that had great promise.

Law reached into an inside pocket of his frock coat, extracted two slim cigars, and tossed one to Covington. By the time they had fired them up, the woman had returned with a mug for the Ranger as well as a fresh pot of coffee. She filled Covington's mug and refilled Law's, favoring him with another lusty look. Then she set the pot in the center of the table and flounced off.

"Looks like you dance card's full for this evening, J.T.," Covington said with a grin and a nod at the woman's retreating back.

"I'm fixin' to make that the case," Law agreed. He raised his cup in a little salute before taking a sip of the hot coffee, which was not the worst he had tasted by a long shot, but was equally far from the best. After blowing out a stream of cigar smoke, he asked, "So what brings you to my supper table, Abe?"

"Got a small job you might be interested in."

"Oh?" Law cocked an eyebrow in Covington's direction.

"Just got a wire from the law over in Fredericksburg. Four boys went and robbed a stage over near there, and made off with a heap of cash. I ain't clear on the details of how much or who the money was meant for. But I reckon it's important to those folks. Anyway, the reward ain't much—only a hundred simoleons each, but since it's been a while since you got back from Big Spring and have recovered, I thought you might like something fairly simple to ease your way back into things."

"Why don't you take care of it, Abe?" Law asked. "Seems

like it's more in your line than mine." He didn't much care
for the thought of chasing four bad men who weren't really
all that bad, apparently, especially when the payoff was rela-
tively small.

"I ain't got the time or resources to go chasin' after these
galoots, J.T. Not with that bunch of Mexican bandidos run-
nin' wild down near Laredo and that spate of rustlin' southwest of here."

Law pondered that for a few minutes, sipping at his coffee and puffing on his cigar. Both men were content with
the silence for the time being. Finally, Law shrugged his
wide shoulders. "Sure, I'll take out after those fellahs," he
said. He had nothing better to do for the next week or so—
which was all he figured he would need to wrap this up.
Plus, Covington had been right—he had not taken on any
jobs in the past couple of months—since he had been
wounded in tracking down some villainous bastards near
Big Spring, and he decided it was about time to test his
mettle.

"Good," Covington said. He pulled some squares of paper from a pocket of his wool vest—a garment that was
stressed to cover the Ranger's bulky torso—and unfolded
them, smoothing them out on the table. With a massive
paw, he slid them across toward Law.

Law stuck the cigar between his teeth and pushed his
mug down, then scooped up the papers and looked at them.
There wasn't much information, just each man's name, a
brief description, and the amount of the reward.

"The man to see in Fredericksburg is the town sheriff, a
feller named Otto Hoffbauer."

Seeing his friend trying with little success to hide a
smile, Law aimed a raised eyebrow at Covington.

The grin spread.

"Abe, you best tell me just what the hell you think is so

goddamn humorous," Law said with a mock growl, "or I'll shoot you down where you sit."

"You ever been to Fredericksburg, J.T.?"

Law shook his head.

"It's a nice place, that town. Settled thirty, thirty-five years ago by Germans. Ain't much strange about that, really. Nor about the fact that the place has been thrivin' mostly from the beginnin'. Those Germans're industrious people. Some of 'em sided with the Confederacy durin' the War of Northern Aggression, but most generally backed the Yankees, so they were under Confederate martial law for most of three years."

"Seems proper," Law said, unconcerned.

"Maybe," Covington commented with a shrug. He grew serious. "But they're basically good people, and from all I've heard, they suffered considerably. Still, they were always a people who kept to themselves. Their experiences durin' the war times only heightened that." The grin crept onto his face again.

"Like I said, them Germans're industrious people, but they are a stubborn lot. Most of 'em're still mighty agitated by their treatment under martial law, so they just flat won't learn to speak our language. Or maybe they've learned it but they just won't use it. Which means, of course," Covington added with an even wider grin, "that when you get to Fredericksburg, you're gonna have a devil of a time tryin' to get any information from the people there."

"That's the real reason you don't want to go chasin' after these fellahs, ain't it?" Law demanded. He wasn't really angry, just a little annoyed that his friend thought he would have to resort to such a ruse to get Law to do this job.

"Nah, hell, that ain't it at all, J.T.," Covington said, looking almost hurt that Law would think such a thing. "Me and the boys're too busy for this. I just think it's a real hoot that you'll have to deal with foreign-talkin' fellers."

"Real hoot," Law snorted. "I ought to kick you right in the ass for this, you evil bastard." He grinned harshly. "I just might have to reconsider."

"Ah, c'mon, J.T.," Covington said, still grinning, "you ain't the kind to go back on your word."

"I am when I been lied to." Then Law smiled. "Hell, Abe, you know I ain't goin' back on my word." He picked up the papers again and looked at them. There were no drawings of the wanted men, just the sparse words. "You know anything about these skunks, Abe?" Law asked.

The Ranger shook his head. "Just what's on there."

Law nodded, folded the papers, and stuck them in a coat pocket. "I'll leave first thing tomorrow," he said. He drained his coffee cup and set it down. "For tonight, though, I'm fixin' to be occupied in more pleasurable pursuits than chasin' two-bit outlaws."

Covington released a big belly laugh, one befitting his size. The chuckle finally petered out. Following Law's gaze, he asked, "You ever consider settlin' down, J.T.?"

"Not since Sara . . ." He stopped, then changed course. "Not in a long, long time, Abe." He smiled, but it was more of a grimace. "Besides, ain't many women going to settle for the likes of me, not with what I do to earn my keep."

"Become a Ranger," Covington said. "Hell, I could get you in, and I'd be right honored to have you. Hell, Billy Tyler'd be thrilled as a drunk let loose in a New Braunfels brewery."

Law grinned a little.

"You'd have steady wages."

"That's true," Law mused with another grin. "I'd get maybe sixty bucks a month to risk my neck doing the same thing I get paid hundreds or even thousands for now. No, thanks, Abe." He grew serious. "Besides, Abe, there'd always be that bit of trouble from Missouri hangin' over me—and it wouldn't look so good for you for hirin' me was that to come to light one day."

"I reckon we could go on back there and get that straightened out," Covington said hopefully.

Law shook his head. "I don't trust those bastards."

"I can understand that. But there ain't no tellin', J.T. You might have call to go back there for something one day."

Law shrugged. "I can't think of a single thing that'd get me to go back there."

Covington accepted that. Rising, he said, "Good luck." He paused, a smile appearing. "I mean, on the hunt for the outlaws, not tonight with her." He nodded in the waitress's direction.

"I reckon luck don't play into that part," Law said with a laugh. As Covington strolled off, Law turned and beckoned the waitress.

As J.T. LAW saddled Toby and loaded a few supplies into his saddlebags, he found himself smiling. He had a purpose for the first time in a couple of months, even if the job was a minor one. And Bridget Haney had been a delightful, inventive, and lusty lover, and the evening had passed in a series of delicious comings together. There had been one final delightful encounter this morning before Bridget had taken her leave of Law's room at the Manor House. Law had then had a leisurely breakfast at Mickleson's, served by a glowing Bridget Haney. Afterward, he had gone to Engstrom's store where he bought a few supplies and then went to the livery.

Within minutes, he had pulled himself into the saddle and was riding out of Austin, heading west. He pushed fairly hard, not that he was in that big of a hurry, but if he was going to run down these outlaws anytime soon, he needed to get to Fredericksburg, where he could pick up their trail. Still, it was afternoon of the third day after leaving Austin before Law pulled into the town of neat homes, busy industries, and bustling shops.

During his ride, he had considered what Covington had said about Fredericksburg, and had concluded that the Ranger's talk about the looming language difficulties was probably just a tale Covington had concocted to irritate him.

But as he rode down the main street of Fredericksburg, he began to see that Covington had been telling the truth—all the signs were in German. Or what he supposed was German. He stopped at a building that had a wooden sign hanging out front under the portico. A star was painted on the sign, along with some words, one of which was Otto. Law figured it was the sheriff's office. He dismounted and tied Toby to the hitching rail, then entered the building.

A short, stout man with thick arms, big hands, and a heavy cropped beard rose from behind the desk. A tin star was pinned to his simple homespun shirt of vertical light-green and white stripes. "Yah?" he said.

"Are you Otto Hoffbauer?" Law asked, wondering what he had gotten himself into here.

"Yah."

"Sheriff of Fredericksburg?"

"Yah?"

"Do you speak English?"

"Yah. Some."

Law nodded. "That's a start," he muttered. Then aloud he said, "My name's J.T. Law." He pulled out the wanted posters and opened them, then tossed them on the desk. "I'm lookin' for those boys. The ones who robbed the stage a couple of days ago."

Hoffbauer made no move to pick up the papers. "You are

a Ranger?" he asked, accent as thick as his bullish neck.

"Nope. Bounty man. My friend, Ranger Captain Abe Covington, asked me to run these fellahs down."

Hoffbauer's face registered disappointment, but he quickly wiped it away. "Dot's goot, I t'ink. You haf done dis before?"

Law nodded, annoyance budding inside him. He saw no need to tell this man that he had been doing this for a long time and that he considered himself to be the best in his profession.

"Den vhy are you here instead of lookink for them?" Hoffbauer demanded.

Law took a moment to make sure his temper was in check. "Wanted to see if there was any more information on 'em than what's contained in those papers," he finally said. "Like where the stage was when it got robbed and which way the bandits might've gone afterward."

"Robbery vas on da road from New Braunfels. Driver said da robbers vent south. Dot's all I know."

Law stared at Hoffbauer for several seconds, then reached out and grabbed up the wanted posters. "You have any more information on these fellahs that ain't on these papers?" he asked tightly.

"Dot is all ve know."

Law stuffed the papers into his coat. "You've been a big help," he said dryly as he stomped outside and mounted Toby. He no longer even wanted to have a meal here; all he wanted was to get out of this town as quickly as possible.

CHAPTER 2

LAW RODE INTO Kerrville late the next morning. At first glance, the town also had something of a German flavor, but Law was relieved to see that most of the signs were in English. He stopped at the small office of town Marshal Emmett Atkins, went inside, and introduced himself.

Atkins—an older man, tall and slender with stooped shoulders, a too-large linsey-woolsy shirt, and a long, shaggy mustache—gave him the once-over, as if trying to decide whether he would dislike the visitor because of what he was.

Law was used to such reactions and took it without rancor, using the time to evaluate the marshal. Atkins appeared to be competent, if not particularly impressive.

"You're after those bad apples who robbed that stage up to Fredericksburg a few days ago, yes?" he asked.

"I am."

"I've been expecting you." Before Law could comment, Atkins said bluntly, "I ain't so sure I approve of bounty men in general, Mister Law. But was you here a couple of days ago, you just might've saved a man's life."

Law's eyebrows rose in question.

"Those boys held up another stage just north of town day before yesterday. Less than a mile away." He shook his head. "Those sons a guns killed Ole Larson, who was ridin' shotgun on the stage, and wounded a passenger."

Law nodded, accepting the information. There was nothing he could do about it now, so he did not concern himself with it. He pulled out the wanted posters and handed them to Atkins. "You have any more information on those boys?"

Atkins didn't even bother to look at the papers, since he knew what was on them. He just dropped them onto the desk, while continuing to stare at Law. "Can't say as I got more information on 'em, but there's more money on their heads now. The bounty's been increased to 250 bucks each." He glared at Law. "Mighty nice raise in pay for a man who makes his livin' collectin' blood money," he commented with a note of disgust in his voice.

"Ain't really all that much for a man who risks his neck to bring such miscreants to heel when folks who wear a star are too lily-livered to do it," Law said flatly.

Atkins was taken aback a little, and at a loss for a response.

"You got fresh paper on these boys?" Law asked evenly.

Atkins nodded and picked them up from where they lay atop a few haphazardly piled ledger books, and handed them to Law.

The bounty man gave them a quick glance before folding them and jamming them into his pocket. He left the ones he had come with on Atkins's desk. "Anything else you can tell me, Marshal?" Law asked politely.

"Not much. The stage driver said he thought Ole wounded one of the sons a guns before he got himself killed. We think they went 'round Kerrville to the southwest. Where they headed from there, I got no idea." Atkins shrugged, suddenly wanting this man out of his office—and his town.

Law nodded, touched the brim of his hat in a good-bye, turned, and went outside. Fall was heavy in the air, though in this area that meant little. Even the winters were mild, something that Law had always appreciated. He glanced up and down the street of the bustling, industrious town. It seemed like a fine place to live and raise a family, he thought, grimacing at the knowledge that it was highly unlikely that he would ever have a family. He pulled out his pocket watch, attached to the fine gold fob, and opened it. He didn't care what time it was; he just wanted a glance at the small, fading photograph inside. It had been a long, long time since he had seen Sara Jane Woodall, but his love for her had never diminished.

With a sigh, Law snapped the watch closed and returned it to the pocket of his black vest. The action opened his coat a bit, revealing the big Colt .45 strapped to his hip and the smaller version in a shoulder holster.

Leaving Toby where he was, Law walked across the street to Jaeger's restaurant. The place was busy, but he found a table near the rear and he sat, back to the wall, keeping a view of the eatery.

A fairly tall, attractive, bosomy young woman with sandy-colored hair stopped next to the table and said something in German.

"Do you speak English?" Law asked, once again irked. He was beginning to feel as if he had been magically transported to another country.

"Oh, yah," the woman said, smiling brightly.

Law took note of what the smile did to her already attractive face. "What do you have?"

The woman reeled off a list of things, virtually none of which Law understood. Finally he held up his hand, stopping her. He smiled. "Just bring me whatever you think is best for today," he said.

"Yah." The blond head bobbed, and she hurried off, long, plain skirt swishing.

Law leaned back and surveyed the room. No one appeared to be dangerous. All the patrons looked like townspeople—shopkeepers and the like. Law figured there was not a single gun among them. He was fully aware that he was being examined, too, though the citizens were not so bold as to make their observations obvious. He thought little of it. With his size, fancy clothes, air of confidence, and the often hard look in his eyes, people tended to cast wary glances in his direction. Plus, in here, he was a stranger, and thus the object of natural curiosity. He ignored the others, except for his natural alertness to any possible danger.

As the waitress came toward him, clutching a large tray laden with his meal, he took off his flat-crowned black hat and tossed it onto the chair next to him, and waited.

The woman set down a plate holding a couple of smoked sausages and a pile of a stringy, sour-smelling vegetable. On a small plate were two thick slices of bread. There were two small crockery bowls, one with butter, another with a brownish-yellow substance.

"What's this?" Law asked, pointing to the item next to the sausages.

"Sauerkraut." Said with another smile.

"And this?" He indicated the brownish-yellow liquid.

"Mustard. You put some on your vurst."

"The sausages?"

"Yah."

Law nodded. "What kind of bread is this?" he asked. "I've never seen it."

"Is called pumpernickel. Is goot."

"I wager it is." He smiled again and received one in return. "What's your name?"

"Elsa." She took the last item from her tray—a glass of dark beer—and set it on the table. "*Guten appetit*—enjoy your meal," she said as she moved off, swinging her hips a bit more enticingly than before.

Law watched until she had disappeared into the kitchen. Then he turned to his meal. He had never had any of these things before, but he was not fussy about feeding. He dug in and was pleasantly surprised at the savory, tart tastes of the meat, sauerkraut, and mustard, and the rich delicious-ness of the pumpernickel. The beer was a perfect comple-ment to it all.

He had another large mug of beer with a cigar after the meal, contemplating staying in town for a while to get to know Elsa better. But he knew he could not do that. So he finally rose and dropped some greenbacks on the table, making sure there was some extra for Elsa. He sauntered outside and across the street, mounted Toby, and rode out of town, heading north.

Law soon found where the robbery had taken place. He dismounted and tossed Toby's reins over the branch of a bush. He paced the area, searching the ground and brush. He found some places where blood had soaked into the ground, but decided right off that it had come either from the stage guard who had been killed or the passenger who had been wounded. Several yards away, though, he found a few drops of what appeared to be blood in the dirt. More searching soon led to a few more spots, then a couple of more, heading southwest. He moved left and right a little ways, looking at the ground, memorizing the hoofprints of the outlaws' horses.

With a nod, Law hurried back to Toby, mounted up, and rode out, moving slowly, eyes scanning the ground, follow-ing the horse tracks and the occasional splotch of blood.

By midafternoon, he came to the Guadalupe River. He sat a moment, wondering which way the outlaws would have gone, then decided southeast, away from Kerrville, would make the most sense. He moved slowly, finally picking out more blood and hoofprints, though both were hard to discern in the brush and grass and mud. Then he lost the trail and stopped. He turned back to where the last certain sighting of the trail was, then eased Toby into the slow but strong current of the river.

On the other side, it took Law some time to pick up the trail again. It eventually led to a cave near a small creek that ran into the Guadalupe River. Law stopped and observed the cave mouth. Though he saw a wisp of smoke now and then coming out of the cave, the shelter did not appear to be large enough, from where he was standing, to hold four men and their horses.

He dismounted. Sticking to the trees and brush, he searched for the trail. He eventually found it, and in studying it realized that there were hoofprints from only three horses. He smiled grimly. There was only one man inside the cave—the wounded one, he assumed. He figured the man must be in bad shape for his companions to have left him.

Law rode back toward the cave and stopped at the edge of the trees overlooking the small cleared patch around the cave mouth. He waited a bit to see if there was any activity. When there was none after a few minutes, he strode quickly across the clearing to the cave mouth, where he flattened himself back against the side wall just inside. He listened intently, but all he heard was the scrape of a hoof against ground and the shaking of a mane.

He pulled out the larger of the Colt Peacemakers, holding it uncocked at arm's length down his leg, and moved forward into the cave. Law did not wear spurs, in part because he thought them cruel to his horse, but more because they were too noisy in tense situations like this one.

As he inched ahead, he wondered if perhaps the outlaw had died from his wound. That would be an annoyance, though not a large one. He would hate to lose out, but he could not in good conscience drag the body back to Kerrville and collect the reward money. On the plus side, if the man were dead, he would be able to get back on the others' trail right away.

The cave made a sharp left, cutting off most of the light from outside. Law stopped, letting his eyes adjust to the flickering of the firelight from ahead. He moved on again, still slowly, and the firelight grew brighter. He could see that, a few yards ahead, the cave widened some. He could still hear soft horse noises but nothing else. He eased up on the widening area and peered around the rock outcropping.

A horse stood near the wall to his left. In the center of the "room" was a small fire. A man lay on a bedroll just to the right of the fire, feet toward Law. He appeared to be asleep, though he might be dead, as far as Law could tell from here.

Law moved forward, heading for the man. The horse suddenly caught his scent and shuffled nervously, feet stamping a little, and it neighed.

The man jerked awake and started to push himself up. Law took two long strides and pressed a boot sole onto the man's chest, pinning him down. Law raised his pistol, cocking it as he did, and pointed it at the head of the man he figured was Mitch Bigelow.

"I suggest you just take it easy there, pard," Law said quietly.

"Who're you?" There was fear in the voice.

"Name's J.T. Law. And I've come to take you back to Kerrville to answer for your misdeeds."

"You ain't no lawman."

"That's right, bub. I'm here for the bounty, and I can take you back alive or dead. Don't matter none to me which. So it's up to you."

"I ain't so sure I'll even make it to Kerrville," Bigelow said.

Law moved his foot. Keeping the pistol aimed at Bigelow's head, he knelt and pulled out Bigelow's pistol and tossed it out of the way. Then he uncocked the Colt and slipped it back into the holster.

"Don't even think of tryin' anything, bub," he warned. "Even on the best of your days I'd swat you down like a fly." He pulled out the knife from the sheath at the small of his back and used it to slit open Bigelow's dried-blood-encrusted shirt.

"Don't look fatal to me," Law said after briefly checking out the wound high on Bigelow's shoulder, just below the collarbone. With a bit of doctoring, it should be fine.

"That ain't what my pards said."

"Your pards ain't much on loyalty if they left you here to die when you're not wounded all that bad."

"They didn't leave me here to die, dammit," Bigelow snapped. "They had some business to see to and will be comin' back for me."

Law gave him a skeptical look but said nothing. He rose. "All right, pard, let's go," he said.

"Not sure I can get up by myself," Bigelow said.

Law figured he was lying, but could see no real reason not to help. He held out a hand.

Bigelow grabbed it and allowed himself to be pulled up. As he rose, he tightened his grip on Law's hand, tried to pull Law toward him, then reached out his left hand and tried to latch on to the Colt in the hip holster.

"Goddamn fool," Law muttered.

CHAPTER 3

LAW RESISTED BEING tugged forward. He swung his right hip back, and Bigelow's hand missed the gun butt. Law swung his right knee up, catching Bigelow in the pit of his stomach.

The outlaw doubled over as his breath whooshed out, and he let go of Law's hand. The bounty man grabbed the outlaw by the back of the shirt and the seat of his pants, and shoved him forward.

Bigelow managed to get his arms up before he slammed into the wall of the cave. He grunted with the impact, though, and tumbled back a step before falling onto his buttocks.

Law jerked out a pistol, ready to put a bullet into the back of the damn fool outlaw's head, but he stopped himself before his trigger finger exerted the small amount of pressure that would have killed Bigelow. He stood there a moment thinking. He had no compunction about killing an outlaw who was responsible for the murder of a stage guard who had died while trying to do his job, though he was highly reluctant to shoot a man in the back. The more immediate concern, he realized, was that if he shot Bigelow, the people of Kerrville might think that the outlaw had died of his original wound and that Law had shot a man who was already dead just to collect the reward. That went against Law's grain. But he wasn't about to give up the reward when he had actually captured the man and brought him in.

Law holstered the pistol. He stepped over, grabbed Bigelow by his long, greasy hair, and jerked him around, then shoved him facedown in the dirt. Kneeling on the outlaw's back, Law whipped off his own black string tie and swiftly lashed Bigelow's hands behind his back.

"Don't move," Law commanded as he rose. He moved off to where Bigelow's saddle and other tack were piled, and grabbed a rope. He cut off a short length, then went back and used that to bind the outlaw's hands, retrieving his tie in the process, which he tied back around his neck.

He effortlessly yanked Bigelow up to his feet and pushed him back toward the fire. "Sit," he ordered. "I told you before not to do anything stupid, bub, and like a goddamn fool, you did. You saw where it got you. You go and try somethin' else against me, and you'll regret it. Got me?"

Bigelow glared at him a minute, then his shoulders sagged, and he nodded.

"Good." Law went to Bigelow's horse and quickly saddled and bridled the animal. He helped the grumbling outlaw into the saddle and used another length of rope to lash his feet under the horse's belly.

"I got nothin' against you, Mister," Bigelow said, voice a little shaky. "But I had to try somethin', you know."

Law looked at him, seeing fear in the man's dirty brown eyes. There was fresh blood on his filthy shirt, the wound having reopened during their little fracas. "Why's that?"

"C'mon, Law, you know damn well that if you take me back to Kerrville, they're gonna hang me sure as hell."

"Reckon that's a fact," Law said easily. He had no sympathy for the man. "But you and your pardners should've thought about that before you went and killed a good man." He had no idea whether Ole Larson was a good man or not, but he wasn't an outlaw, and that was good enough for him at the moment.

"Hell, I didn't kill that man," Bigelow said, trying to sound hopeful. "And I didn't shoot that passenger, neither."

"Who did?"

"I can't tell you that. I'd be a goner for certain. Them boys I rode with ain't noted for their kindly dispensation toward some feller goes against 'em."

"I'd say you got more pressin' concerns right now, bub," Law offered.

"Reckon you're right there, bounty man," Bigelow said gloomily. Then an avaricious gleam leaped into his eyes. "Tell you what, Mister," he added, voice becoming urgent. "I'll tell you who done the shootin'—if you cut me loose and let me skedaddle. I give you my word that I won't never show my face in these parts again."

"Your word don't mean shit to me, bub," Law said flatly. He paused, glaring at Bigelow. Then he continued. "I'll tell you what, though, boy. You tell me who done the shootin'— and you tell me where those other mudsills have gotten off to—and I'll put in a good word on your behalf with the people of Kerrville. I know that ain't much, but it might keep you from gettin' your neck stretched."

Bigelow's hope faded. He should have known this man wasn't the kind to accept such a proposal.

Seeing that Bigelow was not going to answer, Law took the reins to the outlaw's horse and led it outside. He mounted Toby and then, towing the outlaw's horse, rode off, heading north. Before long, he found a ford on the Guadalupe River and eased into it. The two horses made it across without incident. With darkness not far off, Law picked up the pace.

Dusk was just arriving when Law and his captive passed the first buildings on the outskirts of Kerrville. As they neared the main part of town, Bigelow suddenly said, "New Braunfels."

Law pulled to a halt. Turning in the saddle, he asked, "What'd you say?"

"New Braunfels. That's where my amigos were headin'."

Law nodded and started to turn back to the front, but Bigelow's voice stopped him: "You gonna talk to the marshal here?"

"Who killed Larson and shot that passenger?" Law countered.

"Chunk did it."

"Who?"

"Chunk Applewhite."

That registered with Law. "You mean Chester Applewhite?" he asked.

"That's him. We all called him 'Chunk,' seein' as he's a mite portly, you could say."

Law nodded. "He shot both of them?"

"Yep."

"I ain't so sure I believe you, bub," Law said.

"I know that," Bigelow acknowledged. "But I'm tellin' true. He's a mean son of a bitch." He shook his head. "He might've had to shoot that guard, who was about to kill me—tried his damnedest to do so," he added, nodding his chin toward the wound on his chest. "But there weren't no call to kill him. Nor to shoot that passenger. That's put the noose on all our necks."

Law stared at Bigelow for a few moments, then decided the man was telling the truth. "I'll talk to Marshal Atkins," he said before turned back to the front and moving on again.

Minutes later, Mitch Bigelow was safely in Marshal Emmett Atkins's jail, and the doctor had been summoned. As Atkins did the paperwork so Law could get his reward money, Law said, "Bigelow told me it was Chester Applewhite who shot Larson and that passenger."

"You believe that cur?" Atkins asked, glancing up. He was not thrilled about seeing the reward money go to Law, though he was not sure why.

"Yep. He also told me where the others were headin'. I told him I'd tell you that he offered that help. You might want to mention it to the judge."

"Might not, either," Atkins said.

Law shrugged. "That's your concern, Marshal."

WITH THE JUST-EARNED $250 reward in his pocket, Law stopped at the Kerrville Gasthof hotel and got himself a room. After dropping off his saddlebags and rifle in the room, he rode to the livery and made arrangements for Toby's care. Then he walked back up Main Street to Jaeger's, where he took the same table he had had earlier in the day.

He was pleased—very pleased—to see that Elsa was still working. Despite the long day she must have had, she was still polite and smiling brightly.

"I'll have the same thing I had earlier," he said. "But bring the beer first, so's I can have some while I'm waiting for my food."

"Yah. Is goot plan," Elsa said before hurrying off.

Even after serving him his food—and later a second beer—Elsa seemed to hover nearby, apparently ready to leap to his service at his slightest whim. He found it a little disconcerting, but he enjoyed it nonetheless.

Finally Law pushed his plates and mug away. Elsa started stacking the items on a tray. "Kaffee?" she asked.

Law nodded. When Elsa brought a steaming mug of black coffee, Law asked, "When do you finish work here, Elsa?"

"Soon," she responded, her smile dazzling, her blue eyes bright with anticipation.

"I'd like to see you then."

"Yah. I like dot, too."

Law stared into those liquid, lusty eyes a few moments, and realized she needed no more "courting" than he did. "Room twenty-one over at the Kerrville Gasthof," he said.

"Yah, I vill be dere." She flounced off.

Law savored the coffee and a slim cigar before sauntering out of the restaurant and to his hotel room. He hung his holsters on bedposts, and arranged to have his frock coat and dirty shirt cleaned and pressed. He put on a fresh shirt, but left it hanging loose outside his pants. Then he waited.

It was not long before Elsa knocked at the door. She offered a shy smile that belied the desire in her saucy blue eyes as she entered. She had changed into a simple calico dress with a high, modest neck. Her blond hair hung loosely around her shoulders.

Law closed and locked the door, then strode to Elsa, taking her in his arms. His lips found hers, and they devoured each other. Soon they were naked and on the bed, raising a right good ruckus that was no less powerful for its brevity.

Sometime later, Law started to stroke her again, this time taking his time, and relishing the wholeness of her—the fine, strong, body; high, proud breasts; long, shapely legs; sweet face.

IT WAS WITH the utmost reluctance that Law parted ways with Elsa the next morning after a final lingering session of lovemaking. They dressed—Law going out without his frock coat, which had not been returned yet, wearing only a vest over his shirt, pistols in full view—and went to breakfast at a restaurant other than Jaeger's. After dawdling over the meal and coffee, they finally said good-bye outside on the wood sidewalk. As Law turned to head back to his hotel, he knew he would remember this interlude for a long time.

At the Gasthof, he got his clean coat and shirt, packing the latter and donning the former. At the livery, he saddled Toby, then stopped by the general store for some supplies. Then he rode out of town, heading east and a little south.

Though he wasted no time, it still took him three days before he got to New Braunfels, a town that greatly resembled Fredericksburg in its architecture and signage but without—Law was to soon learn—the bitter attitude.

Law stopped at what he thought was the town marshal's office and went inside. A tall, thickset man with a huge black mustache and muttonchops looked up at him from behind a gleaming, clutter-free desk. "Are you the marshal?" Law asked.

"Yah." Said without inflection.

"Do you speak English?"

"Yah, of course. Vhy do you ask dot?" He looked puzzled.

"Well, I was in Fredericksburg just a bit ago and . . ."

"Ah, I understand," the marshal said, cutting him off. "Ve here in New Braunfels are not so unvillink to adapt to new vays." He rose, showing that he had several inches in height on Law's six-foot-two or so, and held out a meaty hand. "Marshal Max Fuhrmann."

Law took the proffered hand. "J.T. Law."

"Sit," Fuhrmann said, indicating the chair next to Law. As Law and the marshal sat, Fuhrmann asked, "Vhat can I do for you, Herr Law?"

Law pulled out the papers and handed them over to

Fuhrmann. "I'm lookin' for these fellahs. I was told they might be headed here, though if they were, they would've been here three, maybe four days ago."

Fuhrmann glanced at the top wanted poster, and his joviality dropped like a rock. His face was hard when he looked back to Law. "You are a lawman?" he asked.

"Bounty man," Law responded flatly.

"I don't usually like such men as you, Herr Law," Fuhrmann said with no apology in his voice. "But I hope you, or somvun, vill catch these *Schweinehunds*—bastards," he snapped, voice angry.

"I take it those boys've been here?" Law said dryly.

"Yah," Fuhrmann spit. "Four days ago. They robbed der bank und killed two men, vun in der bank, the other vhen we chase them vit' a posse. They pinned us down, killed dot vun feller, and stole three horses. I vanted to keep after them," he said, voice suddenly sounding a little defeated. "But the others, they didn't vant to, and I couldn't go on by meinself. Besides, by then they vere out of mein territory. The county sheriff," he added, gaining vehemence again, "vouldn't do nottink. I vired for the Rangers, but der captain said somebody vas on the . . ." His eyes widened. "You are the von he meant?"

"Likely," Law acknowledged. "You wired Cap'n Abe Covington?"

"Yeah, dot is the vun who vired me back." He paused. "I thought maybe he had meant der Pinkertons, a couple of vhich came here two days ago from San Antonio."

"It'll be a cold day in hell when Abe Covington asks the Pinkertons to do anything," Law said flatly. "When he first got word of these bastards, all they had done was rob a stage. He had other, more important business, so he asked me to handle it. We never figured 'em to turn this bad so quick. There was four of 'em to start with. I caught one of 'em—he was wounded by the stagecoach guard before the guard was killed up near Kerrville. He told me the others had headed this way."

"Vell, I vill help you as much as possible. I just vish I could go vit' you."

"I work better alone, anyway," Law said.

"Der revard money is now five hundred dollars each for the three. Should be more, I t'ink."

"Well, get me new paper on 'em, point me in the direction they went, let me get some grub and some supplies, and I'll be on my way," Law said. "They've got a few days head start on me, and if the Pinkertons find 'em, they'll like as not bugger the job up."

"Yah, dot dey vill."

CHAPTER 4

JOHN THOMAS LAW gobbled down a meal at the nearest restaurant, got enough supplies to last five or six days, then paid a visit to the telegraph office, where he sent a message to Covington, telling the Ranger where he was and what had transpired. Then he stopped by Fuhrmann's office to get the new wanted handbills on Chester "Chunk" Applewhite, Huey Bohannan, and Kermit Hanratty. Stuffing the posters in a coat pocket, he rode hard out of town, heading southwest.

A couple of miles out, he slowed, eyes searching the ground for sign of the three horses he had been following since Kerrville. He finally picked them up and took note of the new hoofprints of the horses the men had stolen in New Braunfels. Not long after, he also spotted the tracks of several other horses. He studied them a while and realized that some riders had passed by after the outlaws had. He figured the tracks were made by the Pinkerton detectives. He just hoped they had not found the outlaws. It was a matter of personal pride that he be the one to run these hardcases down. Plus it meant fifteen hundred dollars to him, and that was no small matter, either.

Nightfall found him in Seguin, a small, quiet place but one that seemed hospitable. Seeing a lantern burning in the marshal's office, Law stopped in.

Marshal Otis Reeves, a spare, middle-aged man with thinning hair and a mouse-colored mustache that looked as if it had been attacked by moths, nodded after listening to Law explain why he was there. "A feller southeast of town come in yesterday and said he had seen three hard-lookin' men ride by his farm. From what he said, it sounded like these men."

"Any Pinkertons been by?" Law asked.

"Went through town, but never stopped by here to talk to me," Reeves said flatly. "Which don't make me no never mind. I got no use for them fellers anyway. Damned Yankee outsiders."

"How far behind the outlaws were they?" Law asked.

Reeves grinned a bit. "Likely quite a bit behind 'em by now. Those damn fools rode east out of here. Toward Gonzales."

"And you said that farmer's place is southeast?"

"Right as rain you are, Mister Law."

Law tried to grin but didn't manage too well. He pushed himself up. He was tired, and knew Toby needed care and some rest. "There any place to spend the night here in town?" he asked.

"Only hotel is the Texas Star." He pointed. "Three doors up the street here. Cy McLellan runs a nice place. Even has a small livery behind the hotel. And a restaurant just off the lobby. That might still be open now, but even if it ain't, Cy'll probably see that you get fed."

"Obliged."

* * *

LAW TRACKED THE three outlaws past farms, across streams, and through the town of Stockdale, where he spent the night after leaving Seguin. He followed the trail through Czestochowa and Panna Maria, two towns in which he spent virtually no time, as everyone spoke only Polish, as far as Law could ascertain within a few minutes. Then came other small towns: Pettus, Walton Station, and Beeville. Outside of Pettus, he found a farm family grieving over the murder of the man of the house, killed by the men Law was chasing. The men had raped the farmer's wife, then took what supplies they wanted and rode off.

The trail finally led him to a thicket on the edge of a clearing across which sat a cabin along Poesta Creek. He wondered a little about where they could have been heading, but shrugged it off. It didn't really matter. They were not going another step farther, Law vowed. The only question was how he was going to take these men, but he knew he would find an answer when it was needed.

Just over two hours after he had taken up his perch behind the live oak, the cabin door opened. Law slid the telescope out to its full length and peered through it as a hatless man stepped out of the cabin and ambled with a noticeable lack of concern toward the privy.

As soon as the man—Kermit Hanratty—entered the outhouse, Law snapped the telescope shut, shoved it into his pocket, and moved down toward the privy himself, keeping behind the trees until he had the privy between him and the cabin. He slid up along the side of the outhouse and stopped. Even if someone else came out of the house, he could not be seen. He waited, trying to ignore the noises and smells from inside. When he finally heard some rustling that indicated Hanratty was near through, Law pulled his big Peacemaker.

When Hanratty flung open the door and stepped outside, Law cracked him a good shot alongside the head with the barrel of the Colt. Hanratty let out a sharp hiss, staggered forward two steps, then sagged to his knees.

Law moved up behind him, grabbed his thick hair, and jerked him to his feet, keeping his grip. "Make a sound and you're a goner, bub," Law said tightly.

Hanratty tried to shake his head, but couldn't move it much with Law's grip on it. Still, it served to clear a few of the cobwebs out. "Who the hell are you?"

"J.T. Law. You're a wanted man, and I aim to take you back to the law to pay for your many crimes. Tell you the truth, though, bub, it don't matter none to me whether you're breathin' or not when I hand you over."

Waiting a second to make sure Hanratty was not going to say or do something, Law jerked Hanratty's head, making him turn, then shoved him forward, releasing his hair, toward the trees. Moments after they got there, Hanratty suddenly stopped, whirled, and charged, bending low, at Law.

The bounty man could not move to the side, but he was able to brace himself as Hanratty plowed into him. He was driven back, and fell, the outlaw half atop him, frantically trying to punch.

Law bucked and kicked, managing to flip Hanratty off. He scrambled up before the outlaw could and kicked Hanratty in the side, then the corner of the jaw. Hanratty flopped onto his back. Law moved in and kicked him several more times on the sides, legs, and once in the head. He stepped back a bit, slid out the big Peacemaker, and thumbed back the hammer. It took all of his willpower—and a jolt of common sense—to keep him from pulling the trigger. To do so would alert the men in the cabin. He was sure he could handle them, but it would be dangerous and unnecessary. He uncocked the pistol and slipped it back into the holster.

"Get up, bub," Law growled, grabbing him by the shirtfront and jerking him to his feet. It wasn't difficult. Kermit Hanratty was a small man, slim and wiry with wispy fuzz on his cheeks, jaw, and upper lip. He was probably no more than twenty-two, which Law figured was a pity—Hanratty was not likely to make it until his next birthday.

Law marched Hanratty to a live oak near where Toby stood, placidly munching the grass and brush, and grabbed his rope. Law backed the still-reeling outlaw up against the tree and then tied his hands back around the trunk, cutting off the rope. He wrapped the rope around Hanratty's ankles and the tree, tied that, and again cut off what he didn't need. He took that still substantial section of rope and fastened a slipknot in one end, which he placed around Hanratty's neck. He tossed the other end of the rope over a branch, pulled it fairly taut, then tied it off to another tree nearby. The outlaw was left standing almost on his toes. Any attempt to sit, or even sag a little, would tighten the slip knot and slowly strangle him.

Law moved around in front of Hanratty, who stared at him with dull, groggy eyes. Taking a sweat-and-snot-soiled bandanna out of a coat pocket, he gagged Hanratty with it. "I'll be back soon, buckeroo," Law said dryly. He turned and went off, stopping at his original position. There he stood for a minute or two, staring down at the cabin through the telescope.

He nodded, shut the 'scope, and shoved it into a pocket. It appeared that the portion of the cabin to the left of the door as he looked at it had fewer gaps between the logs. He headed through the trees until he was right behind the privy, then headed into the open, across the clearing, moving fast. He stopped, almost brushing the cabin wall a foot or so to the side of the door.

Law peered through one of the gaps but could see little inside. The light outside was still too bright. He spotted two shadowy figures sitting at a table, talking softly, sipping from a bottle of whiskey they passed between them. He waited.

A few minutes later, one of the men inside glanced at the door. "What the hell's happened to Kermit?" he wondered aloud.

"Worried?" the other countered, sounding a bit sarcastic.

"Only that he's fallen in the goddamn privy and we might have to fish him out to get his share of the loot." He and his companion laughed. Then he stood. "I don't got a good feelin' 'bout this," he said. "I'm gonna make sure he ain't tryin' to take off on us with all the horses or somethin'." He headed for the door.

When the outlaw opened the door and took a step outside, Law grabbed onto his vest with both hands, swung himself and the outlaw—Huey Bohannan, he determined in that split second—around, and smashed Bohannan's back and head against the cabin wall. He jerked the outlaw forward and slammed him back into the logs again, stunning him some. Law kneed Bohannan in the gut, doubling the man over. Then, hearing the other outlaw inside heading for the door, Law yanked Bohannan forward a bit, then wrapped a forearm around the outlaw's throat, holding him in front of him as a shield. He grabbed Bohannan's pistol and pulled it free of the holster.

"Chunk" Applewhite charged outside, got a few steps from the cabin, and stopped when he saw no one in front of him. Hearing a sound, he whirled, raising the pistol he had drawn while still inside.

"Don't, Chunk!" Bohannan shouted as best he could with the battering he had just taken.

Applewhite, either unable to assess Bohannan's predicament in that blink of an eye, or not caring, simply fired, hitting his compatriot three times in the chest and stomach.

Letting the man fall, Law fired Bohannan's revolver four times in return. His unfamiliarity with the gun, however, sent two of the shots wide. The other two, though, punched holes in Applewhite's face. Applewhite went down, dead before he hit the dirt.

Tossing away the outlaw's pistol, Law drew his big Colt and burst into the cabin. He didn't think anyone else was there, but he had to make sure. The place was empty.

Law quickly saddled three of the outlaws' horses and tied the two bodies onto a pair of them. He took all the horses up into the trees; then he cut a now-frightened Kermit Hanratty loose, shackled his hands behind his back, and tied him onto the third saddled horse.

LATE IN THE morning of the fourth day after leaving the cabin, Law and his grisly cargo pulled into New Braunfels. He attracted a fair amount of attention as he rode up the main street and stopped in front of Marshal Max Fuhrmann's office. Law was tired, filthy, and in desperate need of a shave. He had ridden long hours to make the trip, but it still had been a fairly grueling journey. The only spot of trouble, however, was the first night, when he had unshackled Hanratty to let him relieve himself. Hanratty had come out of the trees with a large branch in his hand, figuring to bash Law's head in and escape. But Law had been ready for him and thumped him pretty good. The outlaw had been plenty subdued afterward, seemingly resigned to the fact that he was going to his doom.

Law shoved Hanratty ahead of him into Fuhrmann's office.

The big marshal look up. Eyes wide, he rose. "Dis is vun of them?" he asked eagerly.

"Yep. The other two are outside, hangin' across their saddles," he added grimly.

Fuhrmann smiled. "Dot is goot!" he exclaimed. "Two dead, yet vun left for us to hang." He grabbed Hanratty's shirt and not too gently hauled him toward the cells in back: There was some rustling, a few grunts and what sounded like a couple of thumps, then the clang of a cell door closing and the lock being turned.

Looking pleased, Fuhrmann strode back into his office and sat, indicating that Law should take the seat across the desk from him.

Law remained standing. "You might want to see about those others," he suggested. "It might be edgin' up onto winter here, but it still ain't all that cool, and I been luggin' them corpses for the better part of four days now. They're gittin' purty ripe."

"Yah," Fuhrmann agreed. Her turned in his chair. "Fritz," he called. "Come here." He looked at Law. "Mein deputy," he explained. When Deputy Fritz Mueller came out from the back where the cells were, Fuhrmann said, "There are two bodies on horses out front. The friends of dot *Schweinehund* in the cell. Taken them to Herr Fassbinder. They are to get the cheapest coffins and they vill be buried vit'out ceremony in der back of der cemetery vit' der other *Ungeziefer*— vermin."

When Mueller had left, Fuhrmann said, "Tell me how it vas you come to take those *Abschaum*—scum."

Law explained it quickly, succinctly, finishing with, "I don't mean to seem unfriendly, Marshal, but it's been a long several days, and I'd like to collect my money and get on over to the nearest barber for a bath and shave, then fill my belly and get some rest."

"Yah, I understand," Fuhrmann said, though he seemed disappointed. He stared at Law a moment, then added, "Vhy don't you go haf your bath und shave, then come here again. By then, I vill be done vit' the papervork, und you can be on your vay."

Law nodded, turned, and headed for the door. He stopped and spun back when Fuhrmann said, "Ah, Herr

Law, I almost forgot—I got a telegram a few days ago from your friend, der Ranger. He vas lookink for you."

"Abe Covington?"

"Yah. Dot is the vun."

"Did he say anything in the wire?"

"Only dot he vas tryink to find you, and dot if you came here, I should tell you he vas lookink for you."

A jolt of concern splashed through Law. It was unlike Covington to be looking for him—unless something was wrong. "Where's the telegraph office?" he asked, urgency spreading through him.

CHAPTER 5

LAW GALLOPED INTO Austin, heedless of whomever or whatever had to get out of his way. He brought Toby to a sharp halt in front of Ranger Captain Abe Covington's office and was off the horse before it had completely stopped. He tossed the ends of the reins over the hitching post, not even bothering to wrap them around it, before storming through the door. He pulled up short at the sight of Walter Godfrey Woodall. "What the hell is he doing here?" Law demanded.

Covington, who had glanced up in surprise, reaching for his pistol when Law had charged into the room, relaxed. "Goddamn, J.T.," he said, "you look like hell."

"To hell with that, Abe," Law snapped. "What the hell is he doing here?" Law pointed to Woodall.

Walter Godfrey Woodall was a medium-sized man in his early- to mid-sixties with the paunch of a man who lived well. Graying muttonchops covered the lower half of his face, though his sandy hair was rather thin on his head. Law had not seen him in close to fifteen years, since the bad blood had reached a boiling point between the two men. When the Civil War, as Woodall called it, or the War of Northern Aggression as Law's father, Howard Thomas Law had labeled it, began, Woodall had sided with the Union. Law's father had given Woodall a choice: leave Texas or die. After the war, Woodall returned and, while he was no longer the richest man in Texas, he was a sycophant for the new Yankee government and still well-off. When Law's parents died of fever, it was Woodall who brokered the sale of the Laws' spread for taxes. That had soured Law's relationship with Sara Jane Woodall, and they had parted. Law had seen neither Sara Jane nor her father since.

"He's why I called you here so urgently," Covington said quietly. "Now sit and let him talk. He needs your help."

"My help?" Law said with a bitter, sour laugh. "Not in a million goddamn years." He had ridden hard through the night to make the fifty or so miles from New Braunfels to Austin because when he had wired Covington from there, the return message said it was urgent for him to get back to Austin. Because of that, Law had not had the shave or bath he had wanted. He had barely taken the time to wolf down a meal, giving Toby a chance to rest a bit and have some feed and water and giving Marshal Max Furhmann enough time to finish up the paperwork. Law had collected his fifteen hundred greenbacks, gotten on Toby, and ridden like hell.

"Sit," Covington said sharply to Law. He looked over at Ranger Private Del MacTell, who stood leaning against a wall. "Del, go take Mister Law's horse over to the livery. Make sure he gets the finest care. You tell Lloyd I'll snap him in half if he don't."

MacTell nodded and left, striding on long, thin legs.

As Law sat, tired, bloodshot eyes glaring from Woodall

to Covington, the Ranger captain reached into a desk drawer
and pulled out a bottle of cheap whiskey and three tumblers.

As Covington was doing so, Ranger Billy Tyler entered.
"Heard you were back, J.T.," he said, cheerfully. The jocu-
larity faded when he saw the grim look on Law's face.

Law gave him a curt nod. He liked Tyler considerably,
but he was in no mood for niceties right now.

Covington pulled out another glass, filled all four, then
handed one over to Law, one to Woodall, and one to Tyler.
Each man took a sip.

"Enough with the damned pleasantries, Abe," Law
growled. "I hauled my ass up here quick's I could on your
say-so only to find this son of a bitch here," he snapped,
pointing at Woodall. "What's going on?"

Covington picked up a sheet of thin, crinkly paper and
tossed it lightly in Law's direction. With a questioning
look, the bounty man gingerly picked it up.

"Mr. Woodall brought that in a few days ago."

"So?" Law asked, surprised.

"Read it," Covington snapped.

Law glanced down at the paper, and his breath caught
in his throat. He knew that fine handwriting well, though
he had not seen it in years now. He read silently until he
had finished the entire letter. The first part was generali-
ties, as if the writer was putting off what really had to be
said. Then:

> Things have taken a bad turn here, Papa.
> Oliver disappeared just after the turn of the new
> year and, I'm afraid, has come to some grievous
> harm. Some factions here in St. Joe no longer hold us
> in very high esteem, and the situation is tense. I fear
> that the children and I are in grave danger. Well,
> maybe not just yet, but I fear that soon such will be

the case. I cannot explain any further than that, other
than to say I don't think I can go to the law or even
the private police.

There is, of course, nothing you can do. But I
wanted to apprise you of what was happening here.
That way, should the worst happen and we learn that
Oliver has met with death, or if the danger becomes
too great, and we have to return to you and Mama,
you will have some inkling of what's gone on.

Your loving daughter,
Sara Jane Gibbons

Still holding the letter, Law looked back up at Woodall
and asked, "Why'd you bring this to Abe?"

"I was concerned, of course," Woodall said flatly. "I
thought Mister Covington, being a Ranger captain, could
help find out what's wrong, and perhaps even do something about it," he added with some disdain. He was a man
used to getting his way, and that had not been the case here.

"I told him there wasn't much I could do up in Missouri," Covington interjected, speaking evenly, though he
was not pleased with Woodall's tone. He paused for another sip of the foul whiskey. "I suggested that he hire
Pinkertons or a similar group for the job."

"Because of the wording of my daughter's letter,"
Woodall said, pomposity still strong in his voice, "I can't
trust the Pinkertons, and I don't know the law there." He
grimaced at what he knew was coming next.

"So," Covington said, suddenly relishing this just a bit,
"I told him I knew somebody who just might be able to do
something. And who would be plenty willing to do so."

"Me," Law said flatly.

"Yep," Covington said with a nod. "It took some con-
vincin', but he agreed to it after a spell." Covington had

fought alongside Law during the war and had no fondness for Woodall, and he knew how Woodall felt about Law. But he also knew that Law still loved Sara Jane and would do anything for her, even after all these years. He was also confident that if she was in danger, Law could protect her as well as find out who was endangering her and put an end to it.

Silence descended as the four men each drank a little red-eye. Then Law smiled in a sad way. There was no question that he would not go. "Well, Abe, I reckon I was wrong when I told you there was nothing that'd get me to go on back to Missouri. There is one thing."

"Even though she's married and got younkers?" Covington questioned, ignoring Woodall.

Law nodded.

"When're you aimin' to leave, J.T.?" Covington asked.

"I'd do so right now if I didn't figure I'd keel over like as not before another hour passed."

"Train leaves midmornin' tomorrow," Covington said, making it sound like a recommendation.

Law looked at Woodall. "Train's expensive, and I'd need some supplies and such," he said, almost as if thinking aloud, but directing it at Woodall.

"You'll have whatever you need," Woodall said gruffly. He winced as he went to take another sip of whiskey, and set the glass down. It was foul, and he wanted no more of it.

Law scratched his thick beard. It annoyed him to be unshaven, as well as filthy and wearing dirty clothes. He could use a good scrubbing, as well as a good meal—or two—and, most important, a good night's sleep. Though he wanted to be on his way, the train schedule and his exhaustion made it impossible. He drained his glass of whiskey and set it on the desk. Then he pushed himself wearily to his feet, patently not paying attention to Woodall. "I'll be on that train tomorrow." He turned and headed for the door.

"You want some company when you go, J.T.?" Tyler suddenly blurted out.

Law turned back into the room and glanced at the young Ranger. Law had liked Tyler from the first time they had met. He was young, not much past his majority, and had a youthful appearance, which many people took for inadequacy. But he was a highly skilled horseman, tracker, gunman, and Ranger. Law gave him a questioning look.

Billy shrugged, suddenly uncomfortable, and said, "Even a lone wolf hunts in a pack now and again, J.T."

"I appreciate the offer, Billy," Law said seriously, "but this is none of your affair."

"Hell, I know that, J.T.," Tyler said, his drawl heavier than usual. He finished off his whiskey and put the empty glass on the corner of Covington's desk. "I don't know what's in that there letter," he added, "and I don't know for certain what you got against Missouri, though I can maybe guess. And I know you and Mister Woodall don't get along, though I don't know why. But whatever it is has you more riled up than a starvin' dog in a butcher shop and is fixin' to make you do somethin' you apparently told Cap'n Covington you'd never do. With all that, I figure you just might need a hand you can trust."

"He makes sense, John Thomas," Covington said.

Law swung his gaze to the captain. "You lost your reason, Abe?"

Covington's massive shoulders rose and fell. "Hell, you don't know what you're gonna face up there, J.T. A trusted *compadre* might come in mighty handy."

"But he's a Ranger—a *Texas* Ranger. Folks up in Missouri might not take kindly to a Texas Ranger roamin' around."

"They won't have much to say about a couple of civilians," Tyler said. He reached up pulled off the hallowed star he war. He fingered it, unwilling to give it up. He looked at Covington, some trepidation in his eyes.

"Put that star back on, Billy," Law said gruffly. He was impressed with the young man's determination, but he could not—would not—allow this.

"Do as he says, Billy," Covington ordered, though his voice was soft. Then he grinned. "You can take if off tomorrow when you get on the train with J.T. I'll hold it for you till you get back. You got some time off comin', I reckon. What you do with it is your concern."

Tyler's thin, young face broke into a grin. "I was hopin' you'd say somethin' like that, Cap'n." He looked at Law. "Looks like you got yourself somebody to watch your back, J.T."

Law nodded. Though he didn't show it, he was pleased. "See you in the mornin'." He left.

"NOW *THAT'S* THE J.T. Law I know," Covington said with more joviality than he really felt. He pulled out a chair across the table from Law in the restaurant next door to the Manor House. Law frequented the eatery.

Law simply grunted. He was in no mood for humor. He was too full of concern about what he might find in Missouri, as well as itchiness to be on the way.

"You ordered yet?" Covington asked.

"Just before you walked in," Law responded. He did look more like himself—clean-shaven, eyes clear after a night's rest, a crisp white shirt, clean frock coat, unsoiled vest, neat string tie. His flat-crowned black hat, sitting on the table near his left hat, had been brushed. His hair was neatly combed.

Covington called a waiter over and ordered his own

breakfast, making sure the waiter brought him a mug right off. He poured himself some coffee and gratefully swallowed several large mouthfuls before setting the speckled-enamel mug down. "You gonna be all right headin' up there, J.T.?" Covington asked quietly.

Law nodded. "I'll be fine." His eyes searched the room, alert, as usual. He saw nothing to concern him. "I just want to get there and see what's going on."

They sat in silence, sipping coffee until their breakfast came, and they ate quickly and quietly. Afterward, each lit a cigar and puffed away.

"Well, J.T.," Covington finally said, "I reckon you best be gettin' over to the depot."

Law nodded and dropped the end of his cigar into the coffee cup, where it died with an angry little hiss. When he went to drop some greenbacks on the table to pay, Covington stopped him. He pulled out a wad of bills, peeled two off, and set them on the table. He gave the rest of Law. "That's from Woodall," he said. "For expenses."

Law nodded, took the money, and shoved it into an inside coat pocket. He and Covington rose and headed out together. The Ranger waited on the boardwalk while Law went his room in the Manor House and got his saddlebags and Winchester rifle. Then they walked with purposeful strides to the livery, where Law threw a rope loosely around the horse's neck. Carrying his saddlebags, he led the way out. The huge Covington carried Law's saddle as if it were little more than a small sack of flour.

Billy Tyler was waiting at the station, leaning casually against a wall of the depot, rolling a sliver of wood around in his teeth. His saddle rested on the ground next to his feet, and his bay mare was tied to a hitching post nearby. "Mornin'," he said jovially. He was about to say more, but Law's dark look stopped him.

"Mornin'," Covington responded.

Tyler pushed himself away from the wall and spit out the crude toothpick. He pulled the badge off his shirt and held it out toward Covington. "Don't lose that, Cap'n," he said with a smile that barely hid a deep worry.

Covington took it. "It'll be here waitin' for you to come back, Private Tyler," he said gruffly, trying to mask the feeling he had for the young Ranger.

The train huffed up to the station from the yard, smoke pouring in thick clouds from the locomotive's smokestack. The conductor called for people to board.

Law and Tyler led their horses into a livestock car and made sure they were secure. Then they stowed their saddles and other tack in the same car. Outside, Tyler shook hands with Covington. Wise beyond his years, he understood that his presence was not needed at the moment. He turned and headed for the train car in which he and Law would travel.

"I don't now what you're gonna face up there, John Thomas," Covington said, "but I have every confidence you'll overcome whatever dangers or adversities you come up against."

Law nodded and shook Covington's hand. "Thanks, Abe."

"And, if you end up needin' more help, you wire me right off. Don't matter that me bein' a Texas Ranger carries no weight up there. I'll come a-runnin'."

"Obliged, Abe," Law said. He didn't think that would be necessary, but it was good to know Covington was willing to throw in with him even if was a risk to his career as well as life. He turned and walked toward the train.

"And give my wishes to Sara Jane," Covington called after him.

Law turned back. Seeing the friendly smile in Covington's face, he nodded and then pulled himself up into the train car. He settled into a seat next to Tyler after taking stock of all the other passengers. "You still have time to back out of this, Billy," Law said.

"I'd as soon hump a rabid she-wolf in the midst of a blizzard," Tyler said flatly.

Law couldn't help but grin the littlest bit. "Well, then, boy, you best get comfortable. It's going to be a long trip."

From a coat pocket, Law pulled out a copy of *The Adventures of Tom Sawyer*. A grateful shopkeeper Law had helped a year or so ago had given it to him. He could read, but it was a chore for him. He had always planned to read this book, but he had never gotten around to getting started on it. He brought it with him now because he figured the long, dull train trip would be a good time to work his way through it. Though he got off to a fine start, his attention soon drifted to the possibilities of what he might face in Missouri—and to what he might say to Sara Jane Woodall, or, rather Sara Jane Gibbons, he corrected himself sourly, after all these years. Though he had not seen her in almost a decade and a half, he still loved her, still thought she was the ideal woman. Such thoughts kept him too preoccupied to pay much attention to Tom Sawyer and his friends.

The train chugged its interminable—to Law, though in reality it was a lot faster than it would have been on horseback, and he knew it—way north and east across eastern Texas and into Arkansas. In Little Rock, Law and Tyler changed trains and headed north. On the fourth morning after leaving Austin, they pulled into St. Joseph, Missouri. Without wasting time, they got their horses, saddled them, and found their way to Franklin Street. They stopped in front of the proper house—a small, neat, clapboard place with a porch the length of the front of the house and a small picket fence separating the street from the little stretch of grass leading to the porch.

Law and Tyler dismounted and tied their horses to the fence. Law hesitated a second, then sighed. He strode forward, through the gate, up the three porch steps, and stopped. He knocked on the door.

CHAPTER 6

"HELLO, SARA JANE," Law said quietly. He suddenly felt a tightness squeeze his heart. She was as beautiful as he had remembered. He was not blind, and he could see the changes wrought by time—the crow's feet at the corners of her eyes and full mouth; the sprinkling of gray through her sandy-colored hair, the beginnings of frown lines on her forehead. But her soft hazel eyes were still penetrating, sparkling with life, and even the look of surprise on her face could not conceal her inherent beauty and the fact that she had weathered the years far better than most. Wealth, which had given her an easy life in most ways, had helped considerably, Law figured.

"What're you doing here, John Thomas?" Sara Jane finally stammered.

"Come to see you." Law remembered his hat, and snatched it off. He hadn't been this flustered in many, many years.

"Whatever for?" Sara Jane asked, her perplexity growing.

"Aren't you going to invite us in?" Law countered.

"Us?" Sara Jane was still in shock, and rather confused.

Law nodded in his companion's direction. "This here's my friend Billy Tyler."

"Howdy, ma'am," Tyler said, removing his high-crowned, wide-brimmed hat.

"Of course," Sara Jane said with a shake of the head, trying to recover her sense. "Where are my manners? Come in." She stepped back a bit to fully open the door. When the two men had stepped into the foyer, Sara Jane closed the door—and locked it.

A few feet inside, to the right, was a staircase leading up to the second floor. On the left side of the foyer, across from the bottom of the staircase, was a doorway. Sara Jane led them through it into a sitting room.

To the left was a window overlooking the front yard. On the wall straight ahead was a large, potbellied stove, to each side of which and facing the middle of the room were two heavy, brocade chairs separated by a small table. Making a *U* facing the stove was a sofa of the same brocade material. To the right was a doorway into a dining area. Rugs covered the floors. Bookcases lined two walls.

"Please, sit," Sara Jane said, beginning to regain some of her composure. She still could not figure out why John Thomas Law wanted to see her, but she knew it would come out sooner or later. Besides, she realized with a bit of a shock that it was nice seeing him. That gave her a pang of guilt, which she had to fight down.

Law took the chair nearest the stove to his right, and Tyler took the one next to it. Sara Jane sat in one of the chairs facing the two men. "So," she said, trying to smile but succeeding only a little, "tell me why you've come to see me, John Thomas."

"To help you with your troubles," Law said quietly.

Sara Jane drew in a short, sharp breath. "What troubles?" she finally managed to say.

Law stared at her with a sympathetic expression for a few moments, then said, "Walter asked me to come help you."

Sara Jane gasped again. "My father? How? Why? What . . . ?" She was totally flummoxed.

"Walter went to Abe Covington for help . . ."

"Didn't he join the Rangers after the war?" Sara Jane interrupted.

Law nodded. "Still is a Ranger, a captain now. That's why Walter went to him. Abe told your pa he couldn't do anything himself, considerin' Texas Rangers have no say in Missouri, of course. He suggested Walter hire the Pinkertons, but your pa said he didn't trust them."

"And Mister Covington, being your friend, and knowing me—and our history—suggested Papa hire you?" Sara Jane finished for him. She was stunned that her father would do that, until she realized that he would do anything to help her and the children, including hiring the man with whom—and with whose parents—he had feuded for years.

"Yes'm."

Sara Jane was dumbfounded. She appreciated the offer of help and even—in her heart—was glad to see Law, but she didn't want anyone getting hurt or being put in danger because of her. She suddenly shoved herself up. "I am so forgetful," she said, almost horrified at her lack of manners. "You boys must be half-starved after your long journey."

"We could use a bite," Law allowed.

Before she could respond, two children—a girl of about nine and a boy about three—bounded into the room, raising a ruckus in their youthful exuberance.

"Children!" Sara Jane said sternly but affectionately. "Hush now. As you can see, we have visitors." She paused. "Where's Lemuel?"

"Kitchen," the girl answered.

"Tell him to take you out back to play and watch over you."

The girl stared at her mother for a moment, then bravely marched over to stand in front of a bemused Billy Tyler. "Who're you?" she asked.

"Janie!" the girl's mother gasped.

"It's all right, ma'am," Tyler said. He looked at the girl. "My name's Billy Tyler, Miss. And you are?"

The girl ignored him and moved over to stand in front of Law. "Your name, sir?" she asked politely, if insistently.

"John Thomas Law." He kept a straight face, though he felt like smiling.

"Enough, Janie," her mother said. "Now, you and Walter go get Lem and play outside like I told you. And mind you bundle up good. It's cold."

"Yes'm," Janie said after a moment more of staring at Law. Then she grabbed her younger brother's hand, and the two of them skipped out the door into the foyer.

"I'm sorry, gentlemen."

"Nothin' to be sorry about, ma'am," Tyler said. "She's as delightful as a fuzzy puppy."

"Thank you, Mister Tyler." She waited until she heard the children go outside, then said, "Now, as I was saying, you boys must be famished, so let's see about getting you some food." She headed out to the foyer, turned left, and walked to the kitchen, followed by Law and Tyler.

There was a small table in the kitchen, with four straight-backed chairs. To the left of the kitchen as they entered it was the dining area, with a much larger table and eight chairs—three on each long side and one at each end.

The men sat, and Sara Jane grabbed the ever-present coffeepot off the stove, set it on the table, then put out three china mugs. As Tyler poured coffee for himself and Law, Sara Jane turned to the pantry and returned a moment later with several potatoes, which she proceeded to chop up and then put on the stove. A while later, she went to the pantry again and got a slab of smoked ham, which she set to frying.

When Sara Jane set out their plates, she said apologetically, "Hope everything's all right. I'm not much used to cooking." Shame pinked her cheeks. "I've always had a maid for such, but I had to let her go just recent." The pink deepened. "I was afraid for her when this trouble started, and I . . . I . . ." She reddened. "Well, I wasn't sure I could keep on paying her, either."

The two men dug in and enthusiastically assured her that it was a fine-tasting meal. They fell into silence then as they ate, avoiding for now what needed to be talked about until the meal was over. When it was, Law and Tyler fired up thin cigars as Sara Jane cleared the dishes from the table. Then she refilled their coffee cups, as well as her own, and she sat.

"So, Sara Jane," Law finally said, "tell me what's happened to put you in danger."

Sara Jane sat for a few moments, trying to compose her thoughts. Then she sighed. "I guess I better start a ways back," she said. "Not long after the war, I guess only a couple of months after I returned from Europe," she went on hesitantly, "Oliver—he's my . . . my," she avoided looking at Law, "husband, came to the Austin area with the new government and met Papa. Soon after, he started courting me. We were married a little more than a year later." She risked a glance at Law's face and cringed at the look of pain there. "I'm sorry," she whispered. She reached out a hand to touch one of his, but withdrew it, thinking she would only make it worse.

Tyler fidgeted, uneasy at the personal nature that the conversation had taken. "I'll be in the other room," he said quietly, starting to rise.

"Stay," Law ordered. He figured the worst of the personal

admissions was over, and that Sara Jane would get to the heart of the matter right away.

"Yes, please stay," Sara Jane insisted in her soft, sweet voice.

"Go on, Sara Jane," Law said, fighting to keep the bitterness and hurt out of his voice. He thought he succeeded.

"A couple of years later, just after Lem was born, Oliver, who was a lawyer, had an offer to work here in St. Joe. So we moved here. Last year, he was appointed to the bench."

"He's a judge?" Law said, eyebrows arching in surprise.

Sara Jane nodded. She sighed raggedly. "He was doing well, too. He was well thought of by everyone." She smiled wanly. "Well, everyone but the criminals." She paused. "I don't know everything that went on, of course, but Oliver told me that someone offered him a large bribe . . . I don't know how much, he just said it was substantial . . . to see that five outlaws who were to be tried for a host of vicious crimes would go free."

"Did he take it?" Law asked, trying not to sound judgmental.

"I don't know for sure," Sara Jane said. "But from all that's happened, I would have to guess that he did."

"So these mudsills're free and won't pay?" Law queried. That made no sense to him. If that was true, why would Gibbons vanish? Unless the outlaws were threatening him to get the money back.

"Oh, no," Sara Jane said. "They were convicted. In fact, they're scheduled to be hanged in a couple of weeks."

That might explain his disappearance, Law figured. If the men who were convicted had outlaw partners still on the loose—which seemed quite likely under the circumstances—they would not be happy about having paid a large bribe and being double-crossed. "Why'd he agree to take the bribe in the first place?" Law demanded softly.

"He didn't tell me," Sara Jane admitted. She paused for a sip of coffee. "But I believe he was threatened. I believe they told him to take the money or they would kill him."

"Or you," Law muttered.

Sara Jane nodded. "Or the children." She sighed again, the fear that she usually kept suppressed shooting through her. She fought it back. "Oliver didn't tell me everything, of course, but he did talk some about it just after the men were convicted. A few days later, he disappeared. All he said that morning was that if he were to stay here, it would put me and the children in danger."

"Why?" Law asked.

"He said he was threatened because he didn't do as he was supposed to even though the outlaws had given him the money. I think some of Ellsworth's men really threatened me or the children."

"Ellsworth?" Law asked.

"Tom Ellsworth. He's the leader of the gang, and one of those convicted."

"Does he have partners on the outside?"

Sara Jane nodded. "Oliver said there were five, maybe six of them who weren't caught with the others, though I guess they were minor members, or at least ones who weren't as well known. Plus he has friends and kinfolk in the area."

"Why haven't they just kidnapped one of the young'uns, or even Sara Jane herself, J.T.?" Tyler interjected. "Beggin' your pardon, ma'am, for speakin' so freely."

"It's all right, Mister Tyler," Sara Jane said.

Law pondered that for some minutes, then said slowly, "Those outlaws still on the loose might be the scum of the earth and be as dumb as dirt, but they'd know that kidnaping or killing the wife or child of a judge would bring all hell down on them. Besides, with their leader and his top lieutenants facing a fast-nearing date with the hangman, they have more important considerations right now. Finding . . . Mister Gibbons . . . or even the money, isn't going to help Ellsworth or the others."

"So there's no danger?" Tyler asked.

"Maybe not right now. I expect Ellsworth's cronies're trying to round up some more money to maybe bribe another judge to overturn the convictions. They might try'n grab Sara Jane or one of the young'uns hoping to force . . . Oliver . . . to come out of hiding with the money. But, like I said, that would have every lawman in the state looking for 'em. It'd be a heap easier to rob a few banks or trains to come up with more money. Later, they could look for . . . Mister Gibbons . . . and that money."

"Seems likely, I reckon," Tyler allowed.

"Of course," Law added, "if they can't get those convictions overturned soon and it gets close to the time Ellsworth and his boys are going to get their necks stretched, his men just might come for Sara Jane or the young'uns, which means the danger is going to get greater as the execution nears."

Sara Jane suppressed a shudder. She had known all along that the danger could increase, but she had managed to keep herself from thinking about it because it was too frightening to contemplate. She kept hoping since this began that somehow the situation would be resolved. And, while the worry was as strong as ever, Law's presence gave her renewed hope. She had not been in contact with him for years, but she had heard through letters from family and friends in Texas of the bad times he had had just after the war—and their breakup—and his eventual success as a bounty man. From all that she had heard, he was just the kind of man needed in a situation like this. With that, her spirits lifted a little.

They sat in silence, each with his or her own thoughts, until a knock on the front door shook them from their reveries. Sara Jane's face blanched.

"I'll go see who that is," Law said, rising.

"No," Sara Jane insisted, placing a hand on his arm. Even though he was still wearing his frock coat, the touch sent a shiver of desire through her, which both excited and frightened her. "I'll see to it. I'll not be intimidated from performing my duties in my own house."

When Sara Jane had left the room, heading down the foyer, Law swung around and walked swiftly through the dining room, turning into the sitting room and across it, where he stopped at the doorway to the foyer. Without hesitation, Tyler followed him.

They were only a few feet from the front door and could hear Sara Jane say sharply, "I've told you before, Mister Dalrymple, I have no idea where Oliver has gone off to. Now, good day."

"That's not good enough, Mrs. Gibbons," a male voice said.

"I said good day, Mister Dalrymple," Sara Jane commented firmly. She began to close the door.

Milt Dalrymple placed a palm against the door and shoved it open, knocking Sara Jane back a step.

CHAPTER 7

DALRYMPLE STEPPED ARROGANTLY inside—and right into the muzzle of John Thomas Law's Colt Peacemaker, which the bounty man rested lightly against the Pinkerton's forehead.

"You're a mite short on manners, bub," Law said not unpleasantly, belying the anger that boiled inside him.

The blood drained from Dalrymple's face, but he tried to maintain his bloated sense of authority. "Who the hell're you?" he demanded, though his voice quavered a bit.

"And what business is that of yours, bub?" Law countered.

"I'm a field agent with the Pinkerton Detective Agency," Dalrymple blustered, "and I'm here on an official investigation. Now, if you know what's good for you, my good man, you'll put that gun away and back off, letting me go about my business."

"You are mighty full of yourself, pard," Law allowed. "From where I'm standin' you ain't so much a detective as you are a clap-ridden half-wit." Law ignored the horrified gasp at his language from Sara Jane behind him.

"You're making a big mistake here, mister," Dalrymple blustered.

"Not nearly as big a mistake as your knotheaded pardner back there behind you is about to make."

"Ned," Dalrymple said hastily, "whatever the hell it is you're aimin' to do, just put a stop to it."

Ned Rogers moved his hand away from the pistol he carried in a holster high up on his right hip, under his town coat, of which only the top button was fastened.

"That's better. Maybe you ain't as dumb as I thought, Ned," Law offered. "Now why don't you ease on in here where we can keep an eye on you."

Rogers did as he was told, squeezing past his partner until he was next to him just inside the door. He found himself staring at a tall, thin, determined-looking young man holding a cocked .44-caliber Remington on him.

"What now?" Dalrymple asked. Most of his bluster was gone, but he still tried to sound as if he were in charge.

"What's gonna happen is you and Ned the pinhead are gonna take your leave of this place and never darken Mrs. Gibbons' "—he almost choked on those words—"doorway again. She has told you she does not know where Mister Gibbons is. If she finds out, and thinks it's important for you to know, she will inform you of it. Until then, keep away from this house, her person, and her children."

"Or what?" Dalrymple asked with bravado.

"Or the Pinkerton Agency will be short one"—his eyes flickered to Rogers and back—"or perhaps two of its finest detectives." He saw no reason to disguise the sarcasm in his voice. "Is that clear?"

"It is," Dalrymple acknowledged after a short stretch of silence.

"Good." Law reached inside Dalrymple's coat and pulled out his pistol. "You have another piece on you?" he asked.

"No," Dalrymple responded in a strangled voice.

"Billy," Law ordered, "relieve Mister Ned there of his pistol, empty it, and then give it back to him. And check to make sure he's not holdin' another piece."

He waited patiently until that was done. Then he removed his pistol from Dalrymple's forehead, much to the relief of the Pinkerton. Law slid the Peacemaker into the holster, opened the loading gate of the .41-caliber Colt Lightning, and ejected the cartridges, one at a time. They fell with little clinks on the floor. Law handed the empty revolver back to Dalrymple.

The Pinkerton took it and glared at Law. Dalrymple was not nearly as tall or as broad-shouldered as Law, but he was solidly built. His face was clean-shaven, revealing a square jaw, and the hard, flat eyes bespoke a meanness that was belied by his fancy town suit, silk vest, and derby.

"Now you mind what I said, Mister Dalrymple," Law said, once again sounding quite pleasant. "Good day to you, sir." He turned to Rogers. "And to you." He shut the door firmly behind them, barely giving Rogers enough time to get out.

Law turned and smiled at Sara Jane. It still pained him no end that she was married to another man, one who apparently had gone bad and abandoned her. But he was determined not to let her see his hurt, though he was aware that he had already failed in it. He did, however, renew his internal vow to keep it from her.

"Thank you, John Thomas," she said, relief easing the worry lines on her face.

"My pleasure, ma'am," Law said with a soft smile. Then his face hardened. "Have the Pinkertons been bothering you?" he asked with distaste. He had never liked them, seeing the Pinkerton Agency as a national Yankee police force that often operated above the law and harassed good people simply because those people were—or at least had been—Southern sympathizers.

Sara Jane nodded. "Some. A day or so after Oliver disappeared, a couple of 'em came 'round. They said they knew about the bribe and wanted to know where Oliver had gotten off to. I told them I didn't know where he'd gone, but they didn't believe me. Since then, they show up now and again asking me where Oliver is and hinting that I face arrest and prosecution if I don't cooperate."

"Well, I reckon we just put an end to that," Law said firmly.

Hearing the children getting a bit too loud from out back, Sara Jane turned and headed toward the kitchen and the door to the backyard.

"You really think them two galoots'll keep their distance from Miz Sara Jane?" Tyler asked when the woman was gone.

"I don't reckon so," Law answered. "Both of 'em are a mite thin between the ears, I'd say, so they won't listen."

"What're you plannin' to do about it?"

Law shrugged. "Ain't sure yet."

"Maybe you should go talk to the man those dunces work for," Tyler suggested.

"Maybe I will," Law lied. There was no way he was going to enter a Pinkerton agency office in Missouri on his own volition. Even for Sara Jane. Unless, of course, it meant life or death for her or her children. It wasn't just that he hated the Pinkertons; it was simply too dangerous for him, considering his past in this area.

Tyler knew something was wrong, and he suspected that Law was lying. Trouble was, he didn't know why. "Maybe I'll just mosey on over there myself," he allowed.

Law cocked an eyebrow at him.

Tyler shrugged and offered a small smile. "There's times

when a man's got to grab his friend's bull by the horns and twist the devil out of it."

Law couldn't help but smile. He had always gotten a lift from Tyler's strange, colorful expressions. He nodded.

"I don't know what's in your past here, J.T.," Tyler said with some hesitation. He didn't know if he should say anything, but he felt he had to. "But if there's anything I can do to help, you only have to ask."

"Obliged, Billy," Law said. He was rather uncomfortable. "But I don't know as if . . ."

Sara Jane entered the back door, herding her three children before her, and came into the foyer, where Law and Tyler still stood. She shooed the two younger children upstairs, then said, "Gentlemen, this is my son Lemuel. Lem, this is Mister Law and Mister Tyler."

"Pleased to meet you, Lem," Law said, shaking the twelve-year-old's hand.

Lemuel's head bobbed and he turned to shake Tyler's hand, nodding again, intimidated by these two men, who appeared to be so much different from his father. He turned and headed up the stairs after his siblings, a skinny boy, all legs and knees and elbows.

"Please, John Thomas, Mister Tyler . . ."

"Billy, please, ma'am."

"Billy," Sara Jane smiled. "Both of you go on back to the kitchen and have some more coffee while I tend to the children for a spell." She turned and went up the stairs.

At the kitchen table, Tyler poured coffee for himself and Law. Grinning, he said, "Wish we had us a snort of coffin varnish to embellish this jamoka."

"Would be a fine thing," Law allowed. He was still distracted. Seeing Sara Jane again after all these years, plus learning of what the trouble was—and wondering what he could do to resolve the situation—had his mind tied up pretty well. He absentmindedly lit another thin cigar and sat there puffing away and sipping coffee, letting his mind work over all the new information.

He had come to no conclusions by the time Sara Jane came back. He shook himself out of his preoccupation and offered a small smile at Sara Jane.

She returned it and sat, suddenly looking tired.

Law sat silently, not knowing what to say to this woman, whom he had loved for so long. Finally, though, he asked, "You have a barn or some other outbuilding, Sara Jane?"

"Yes," Sara Jane said, surprised. "We have a barn. We keep a couple of carriages there, and a pair of horses. Why?"

"Reckon it might be good if Billy and I stayed there," Law said.

"Wouldn't you be more comfortable at a hotel?" Sara Jane countered. "There are several fine establishments in St. Joseph."

"Sure, we'd be a heap more comfortable," Law agreed. "But if we're stayin' in a hotel, we can't watch over you and the young'uns."

"Do you think that's necessary?" Sara Jane asked, some of her fear returning.

Law hesitated a moment, then said, "Maybe not necessary, but I do think it'd be wise. I don't think the danger is great right now, but I can't be certain of that. There's no tellin' what some bad men will do. If me and Billy're right here, we can watch over you and the children."

"For how long?"

"As long as it takes," Law said flatly. Seeing the worry creep back onto Sara Jane's face, he quickly added, "I don't think it'll be long before all this gets straightened out."

Sara Jane nodded. "Of course you may stay in the barn, but wouldn't it be better if you two stayed in the house here? That would offer even more protection." She wasn't all that concerned about herself, but when it came to the children, she would do just about anything for their well-being. She had lost one child before the daughter had turned three; she was not about to lose another if she could help it.

"That would sully your reputation," Law said.

"I don't care about that if my children are in danger," Sara Jane said firmly.

"I know that, Sara Jane," Law said soothingly. "But having two unrelated men in your house when your husband is missing will cause people to talk. And, while you might not care a hoot what they think, it could, somehow, make the situation worse." He held up a big hand, stopping her from protesting. "I don't know how, Sara Jane," he said patiently. "It's just not a risk we need to take."

Sara Jane knew better than to object at this point. She nodded. "If you need anything, you just tell me, John Thomas," she said.

"We'll be fine, Sara Jane," Law said. He rose. "But we best get our horses into the barn and tend to them." He looked around, as if searching for something.

"What're you missin', J.T.?" Tyler asked.

"Where the hell did I put my hat?" he responded, annoyed at himself.

"In the sitting room," Sara Jane said. "You—and Billy, too—tossed your hats on the floor when you sat there just after arriving."

"Ah," Law growled. He and Tyler got their hats and went outside. They rode around the corner of the street to the alley that ran behind the house and turned into the barn, where Sara Jane was waiting for them, shivering in the cold with only a light shawl over her shoulders. As soon as they were inside, she went back into the house. Law and Tyler silently began unsaddling their horses, then currying the animals.

"Maybe you should go talk to the Pinkertons tomorrow, Billy," Law finally said.

"You won't be goin'?" Tyler looked over the back of his

bay horse, resting one forearm lightly on the animal's back near the neck and the other on the rump. He wasn't much surprised. He still didn't know why Law didn't much care for Missouri, though he figured it must be a good reason.

"I don't reckon that'd be wise," Law said flatly. "Besides, I have something else to do." He did not want Tyler along with him when he went looking for information. He probably would have to go to places that would bother Tyler, seeing as how he was a Texas Ranger—even without the badge at the moment—and a lawman down to his socks.

Tyler wondered about that, but nodded. "Sure, J.T.," he said.

Law stopped his work for a moment and said grimly, "You let them Pinkerton worms know for certain that if they bother Sara Jane or her family again, they will pay dearly for their transgressions."

"All right, J.T.," Tyler said, even more baffled than before. *He must be carrying a powerful lot of hate for the Pinkertons*, Tyler thought. *One day I'll have to find out why.*

Law went back to caring for Toby, and gave his friend a half smile. "Just don't mention my name to them," he allowed.

Tyler's surprise and confusion deepened. But he nodded.

The two were soon done with their tasks, then gave the horses a nosebag each of oats and made sure the animals had water. As they were finishing that, Sara Jane entered the barn and announced that another meal would be ready soon.

After supper, the three sat around for a while talking, avoiding for the most part the situation that had brought them together. Being tired from their long journey to get here, Law and Tyler soon said their goodnights and headed for the barn.

* * *

LAW ROLLED OUT of his blankets, Colt in his hand, cocked, before he was even fully awake. He ended up on one knee, gun arm extended. He sucked in a sharp breath as he forced himself to keep his trigger finger from exerting that tiny bit of pressure that would have sent the intruder to the grave.

"Goddammit, Sara Jane!" he snapped, breathing hard as adrenaline pumped through his body. "I damn near killed you." He was almost shaking as he stood, uncocking the revolver and lowering his arm. He glanced over at Tyler, who was almost as rattled. He, too, was just lowering his pistol.

Sara Jane stood in the doorway of the barn, terror on her face.

"What's wrong, Sara Jane?" Law demanded, a jolt of worry shooting through him as the thought that something might have happened to one of the children hit him.

CHAPTER 8

"I'M SORRY," SARA Jane gasped, still trembling.

"It's all right, Sara Jane," Law said quietly. He wanted to take her in his arms and make her fear and worry go away. But he could not. It would not be right, and he was not certain that she would even like or accept it. So he stayed where he was.

The silence grew for some moments, then Law finally asked, "So what's wrong, Sara Jane?"

"They've escaped!" she said, suddenly remembering why she had come here. The past few seconds had startled her.

"Who's escaped?"

"The five men who . . . the ones . . ."

"Ellsworth and his men," Law finished for her.

"Yes," Sara Jane said with a frightened nod.

"Well, don't you fret now, Sara Jane," Law said. "Me and Billy here'll make sure you and the children are safe." He didn't like this new development. With Ellsworth and his top men on the loose, the danger to Sara Jane and the children increased considerably. But he could not change the facts, so he would have to deal with it as best he could.

"What'll we do, John Thomas?" Sara Jane asked, wringing her hands. She had always called him John Thomas, though on rare occasions she might drop the Thomas.

"First thing is you're going to go on back inside and fix us up some grub. Billy and me'll be along directly. We'll need full bellies to face the day."

When they had eaten and were sitting with a final cup of coffee, Law said, "I reckon you should keep the children out of their schoolin' for the next couple of days. They do attend classes, don't they, Sara Jane?"

"Yes. Their schooling was done for the day yesterday when you arrived." In some ways, it seemed like days since Law had shown up at her door.

"Well, I don't suppose Lemuel will much mind missing a few days of sitting in that school," Law said, trying for a little levity. He glanced toward the dining area, where the three children sat, the two younger ones still picking at their meals, Lemuel looking annoyed at having to sit with his younger siblings.

"Nor will Janie," the girl's mother said with a sigh. "Neither is excited about learning numbers or reading."

Law nodded, understanding. "Either Billy or I—or both of us—will be here at all times. If you or the children must go out for any reason, one of us will take you. Do you have any need to leave the house in the next day or so?"

Sara Jane sat and thought about it a few moments, then nodded. "I'll need to visit the mercantile store. I am short of several food items and more."

"Billy has an errand to run straight off," Law said evenly. "Once he's returned from that, I'll escort you to whatever establishments you need to visit."

Sara Jane nodded and left to see to the children. When she was gone, Law turned to Tyler. "When you talk to those goddamn Pinkertons," he said quietly but firmly, "give 'em the warning as I told you. But add this—tell them that with the escape of these hardcases, Sara Jane and her young'uns're in powerful danger. Tell the Pinkertons that we'll shoot anyone who approaches Sara Jane's family. We won't wait to see if they're Pinkertons or local lawmen— or goddamn outlaws."

Tyler nodded.

"You all right with that, Billy?"

"Yessir," Tyler said firmly. "I got no reason to drop my drawers for the pleasures of the Pinkertons."

Law fought back a grin.

"I don't know what you got against the Pinkertons, but your dislike of 'em is good enough for me, I reckon. I've run across 'em a few times down in Texas, and I can't say as if they've ever done anything to endear themselves to me. I reckon they are a mulish lot, though, from what I've seen and heard of 'em."

"Tenacity isn't always a virtue," Law said flatly. "It can lead a man to do some damn fool things at times."

Tyler gave him a questioning look, wondering what his friend meant by that.

Law simply smiled enigmatically.

"You talkin' about you?" Tyler asked. "Or the Pinkertons?"

Law responded with another mysterious smile. "I'm obliged for you takin' on this task, Billy."

LAW PROWLED THE house while Tyler was gone, itchy to be doing something, trying to keep his mind off thoughts of Sara Jane and his still-strong feelings for her. He had wondered all the way on the train ride what he would feel when he first saw her again after all these years, especially since she had been married a long time and had several children. But the years, the complications, the marks of passing time had not dampened his love, he had found. He could not help but wonder what—if anything—she felt for him. There were times in the less than a full day he had been here that he thought he could detect a spark of their old love in her eyes, but he couldn't be sure. When he tried to think clearly about it, he often put it down to his own wishes and desires—that he was seeing in her eyes what he wanted to see there.

Because the children were around—though Sara Jane made sure she and they stayed out of his way—Law kept his frock coat on. The young ones early on had displayed considerable interest in his Colts.

He was relieved when Tyler finally returned, and they met in the sitting room, near the fire—Tyler was pretty cold from being outside. Neither man had brought any cold-weather gear, something that Law cursed himself for, as he should have thought of it.

"It seems those horses' tails ain't much disposed toward heedin' the warnin'," Tyler said. "I swear, most of them Pinkertons're probably dumb enough to kick a cow chip in August while they're wearin' their Sunday shoes."

"They give you any trouble or just tell you they'd go ahead and do whatever it is they feel like?"

"Just the latter, I reckon. Though they were adamant about it. I thought for a spell I was gonna have to shoot my way out of there. They are a hardheaded bunch."

"Reckon they are," Law offered. He thought for a moment, then he shook his head in annoyance. "Damn, I should've never sent you over there to talk to those wretched devils."

"Why not?"

"I knew they were stubborn to a fault, and I should've realized that issuin' them a warnin' like this'd only ruffle their feathers. They'll likely be even more pestiferous than before because of this. And that could be dangerous."

"How so?" Tyler asked. "They won't want to hurt Miz Gibbons or the children."

"I ain't so sure about that," Law said, almost to himself.

"What's that mean?" Tyler questioned, confused.

"Tryin' to flush out a couple of outlaws a few years back," Law muttered, "a bunch of Pinkertons tossed a small bomb into a house. Killed a young boy and blew the arm off Frank and Jesse's mother . . ." He realized he had said too much and snapped his mouth shut.

"Frank and Jesse?" Tyler asked, shocked. "As in Frank and Jesse James?"

Law just glared at his friend.

"It almost sounds like you know 'em," Tyler pressed. He might be young and full of admiration for men like Law, but he was a hardheaded fellow, too, in his own way. When he got no response beyond the continued stare, he pushed harder. "Wait a minute. They rode with Quantrill or Bloody Bill back in the Late Unpleasantness, didn't they?" It was more musing aloud than asking. "So did you, right?"

Law gave him one last glare, then spun and walked out of the room.

Tyler stood there, watching Law's back until it disappeared. He was somewhat shocked, though he supposed after a moment that he shouldn't be. A lot of good men fought unconventionally in that war—including Captain Abe Covington. Still, it seemed to him that there was something more between Law and the Jameses. That might, Tyler figured, explain some things about Law's past. Not that it mattered. He walked to the kitchen, where Law was just telling Sara Jane to get ready to leave.

"You were right, J.T., about how bein' stubborn can lead to a man doin' some damn fool things. Like stickin' his nose into the business of a good friend—and a man he admires a considerable lot—where it don't belong. I'm sorry, J.T. I overstepped my bounds and feel right terrible about it."

Law stared at him in a not unfriendly way for some seconds, then nodded and offered up half a smile. "No harm done, Billy," he said, clapping the younger man on the shoulder. "But mind this—some fellahs don't take kindly to folks pryin' into their past, no matter how good a friend they might be."

Tyler hung his head, abashed. He knew that, of course, and was quite ashamed that he had forgotten it, especially with a man he admired as much as he did Law. On the other hand, it was because of his affection for the bounty man that he had pried. He couldn't help but want to know more about a man he so looked up to.

Law squeezed Tyler's shoulder. "Buck up, boy," he said. "I know you ain't the kind to make such mistakes very often." He paused. "Now," he added, dropping his hand, "I want you to pay attention to front and back while me and Sara Jane're gone, make sure the Pinkertons don't come here in a group to cause some of their deviltry."

Tyler straightened his back and nodded. He would not let Law down—or disappoint him—again.

Law headed out to the barn and hitched one of the Gibbonses' gray geldings to the small surrey. Then he got Sara Jane. Before he could help her up into the carriage, she had climbed up on her own, and they headed into town. Because he had not brought winter clothing, Law was wearing just his frock coat and vest. It was quite cold, but nothing he could not bear for a short while. They clopped slowly down to Main Street, quiet for the most part, not knowing what to say to each other.

Law pulled up in front of Bzovys' Mercantile and hopped down. He spun, wanting to make sure he could help Sara

Jane. He placed his big hands around her waist and lifted her easily down. Despite the fact that her waist was no longer as tiny as it had been when they had last seen each other and despite the heavy cloak she was wearing, the touch sent a shock through him. As he set her down on her feet, he wanted nothing more than to pull her to him and kiss her hard.

But he managed to let her go without doing something that would have embarrassed them both. Again, though, he thought he saw a look of mutual desire in her eyes.

With a glance around the street, Law led Sara Jane inside the store, which was not busy at the time. The place was packed with goods. Alongside the right wall were all manner of hardware and farm implements; along the left were clothing and some dry goods. Hats hung from the ceiling. There was a large stove in the center of the place, in front of which was a small table and several chairs. Though unoccupied now, old men often sat there and played checkers while arguing over . . . anything that came to mind. Scattered around the room were heaps of items like sacks of flour or beans or coffee, as well as tables laden with bolts of cloth, fashion books for the townswomen to look through at their leisure, blankets, Bibles, toys, and a plethora of food items, from salt to cheese to bacon. On the counter were glass cases with cigars, needles, thread and thimbles, spices, penny candy, and more. Behind the counter was a variety of canned goods.

"Mornin', Miz Gibbons," the couple behind the counter chimed in unison. They were a handsome couple of slightly less than average height with compassionate, friendly expressions. The spryness with which they moved belied the fact that they were in their seventies.

"Good day, Mister, Miz Bzovy." Sara Jane smiled a little, perked up by the Bzovys' brightness and warmth. "Folks, this is Mister Law," she added. "John Thomas, this is Ed and Marge Bzovy, the owners of this establishment."

Law shook hands with Bzovy and tipped his hat to Marge. "Pleasure, folks," he said.

"Mister Law is an old friend come to help my family in these perilous times," Sara Jane said.

"Lots of folks will appreciate that," Marge said, looking at Law. "Judge Gibbons and his family are well thought of."

Law smiled crookedly and nodded. He looked at his former love. "Go on about your business, Sara Jane," he said. "I'll be back out of the way keepin' a watch on things." He drifted toward the corner at the right front of the room, near the hardware. Though it was close to the large window in the front wall, the light really did not reach into that corner. He stood, alert, watching out the window, as the Bzovys—under Sara Jane's direction—moved about, gathering up food items.

Minutes later, two hard-looking men walked in, sauntering arrogantly toward the counter. They stopped when they saw Sara Jane. In the corner, Law stiffened, ready for trouble.

"Be right with you boys," Marge said cheerfully.

The two men mumbled some response, but continued to stare at Sara Jane for several moments. They whispered between themselves a bit. Finally they nodded to each other. "We'll be back," one said, and they left.

Law turned and watched out the window again. The two men stopped near where Sara Jane's surrey was hitched parallel to the boardwalk. They turned and faced the store, thumbs hooked in their gunbelts, which they wore outside heavy cloth coats. They waited.

Law marched over to where Sara Jane was talking with Marge. "There a back door, ma'am?" he asked.

"Of course," Marge said. She was unflustered. "Just go on back and through."

Law nodded. "Stay here, Sara Jane," he said as he spun

on his heel and headed behind the counter, though the storage room at back, and outside. He turned right and hurriedly walked down past the pharmacy next door, turned again on the small street there, to the end of the building, where he stopped and peered around the corner. The two men were still there, watching the front of the store.

Law moved out into the middle of Main Street and walked up toward the store. He stopped a few yards behind the two men. "You boys waitin' for someone?" he asked.

CHAPTER 9

THE TWO MEN swung toward Law, annoyance and alarm writ on their faces. When they saw they faced only one man, they relaxed a little, though they remained wary.

"You talkin' to us, mister?" one of them asked, assuming an air of innocence.

"Yes, I'm talkin' to you two dumb cusses," Law said with a touch of sarcasm.

"I don't see where that's any of your concern, mister," the same man said. Like the other, he was a few years younger than Law's late thirties. He was of medium height and had a chubby face that was mostly covered with dull brown stubble and a thick mustache. Hair of the same color spilled out of his hat over his ears and on his neck. His coat was a dingy brown and somewhat moth eaten. Like his partner, he wore a gunbelt outside his coat, holding two pistols, one on each hip.

"There ain't but one person shopping in that store right now, and I know for goddamn certain you ain't waitin' for her," Law said roughly.

"Now, look here, mister . . ." Brown Coat started.

But his partner cut him off. "Shut up, Clyde," the other man said. "You go to hell, mister. I don't know who the hell you think you are, but you're stickin' your nose in business that don't concern you. Now, if you got any sense at all, you'll be on your way."

Law turned his hard gaze to that man. He was a bit taller than his partner, and clean-shaven, though he, too, sported a thick, bushy mustache. His was black, matching the straight hair that hung well past his shoulders. His coat was the same rump-length cloth garment as his friend's, but of a faded black color. Law thought he recognized the man but could not place him.

"I reckon not, bub," Law allowed. "And if you and your donkey-faced pard over there got any sense, you'll both mosey on and forget whatever deviltry you're fixin' to make here." He pushed back the right side of his frock coat, tucking it behind him, so the walnut grip of the big Colt Peacemaker was accessible.

The two hardcases stared at him, their breath frosting in the cold air. All three men ignored the small crowd that had gathered warily nearby, interested but staying back a bit for safety's sake.

Black Hair and Brown Coat looked at each other, then back to Law. Black Hair shrugged. "Maybe you're right, friend," he said, putting on an air of friendly surrender. "Not that we was plannin' any mischief. Hell, we ain't meanin' no harm to no one. But I expect we don't need no confrontation here."

Law said nothing, nor did he move. He just continued waiting, eyes alert.

The two looked at each other again, then turned and strolled away, moving a little apart as they did.

As soon as the two had started walking off, Law had slid several paces to his left, certain they would try something.

He just hoped no innocent bystander would get shot when they did.

Black Hair and Brown Coat went only a few yards before both stopped and spun, jerking out pistols. Each man fired twice, then stopped, realizing that Law was not where he had been moments before.

While they cast panicked eyes around, Law calmly pulled his large Colt .45. "Over here, boys," he said, voice carrying well in the quiet that had descended as the echoes of the gunshots faded.

As the two gunmen turned in his direction, Law squeezed off five rounds. Two slugs slammed into Brown Coat's chest and another into his plump face; one hit Black Hair high in the abdomen, the other up on his right shoulder.

The winter wind pushed the gun smoke away quickly. As Law began walking toward the two sprawled men, he ejected the spent shells from his Colt and reloaded it. He was finished when he reached Brown Coat. The man was dead. Law took the few steps to Black Hair, who was still alive, but Law figured he would not last long. He knelt next to the man, his feeling of recognition stronger. And he thought he remembered why.

"You used to ride with Frank and Jesse, didn't you?" Law asked.

The man coughed a bit, spitting up a little blood. "Yep," he said, breathing ragged. "But they've been layin' low for a couple of years now, especially Jesse." He paused. "I hear him and Frank are livin' under fake names down in Kentucky."

"What've you been doing?"

Black Hair tried to shrug, but it only produced another spate of coughing. "When Frank and Jesse went to ground, I started ridin' with Tom Ellsworth. Hell, ain't much an ol' cuss like me can do. After ridin' with Bill Quan . . ." His eyes widened. He coughed up more blood. "You were one of us," he gasped.

Law nodded. With his memory jogged, he managed to put a name with the face. He had still been pretty young when he'd joined up with Quantrill's Raiders near the end of their run. "You're Dick Bailey?"

"Yep." His breath was coming in jagged bursts.

"I know you and your damn fool partner were after Mrs. Gibbons, but why would you think to try to take her out in broad daylight with a passel of people around?" Law asked.

Bailey tried to answered, but all that came out was a small cough, then a final exhausted sigh. Bailey was dead.

Law wasn't all that worried about it. As far as he was concerned, Bailey had gotten what he had deserved. But Law thought it would have been nice to have gotten some answers. He reached out his left hand and gently brushed Bailey's eyelids shut. As he was doing so, he caught movement—a man or men were coming at him fast.

Still kneeling, he swung in that direction, raising the Colt as he did. When he saw the silver stars, he slid his finger off the trigger and rested it along the trigger guard, but he did not lower the weapon.

The approaching men—three of them—stopped when they saw that big Colt pointed at them. All three had their own revolvers out, aimed at Law.

"I'm Marshal Al Fairburn," the man in the lead said. "Drop your piece and submit."

Fairburn was several years older than Law, rather short, but powerfully built. A straw-colored mustache drooped around his upper lips and hung off his chin by several inches. He was hatless, as were the other two men—Fairburn's deputies, Law assumed—and had no coat, only a vest. Law figured that when he and his deputies heard the gunfire, or were alerted to it, they just ran out dressed as they had been. A shock of hair, parted in the center and the same color as the mustache, hung almost to his shoulders.

Law rose, but the Peacemaker in his right hand never wavered. His rise had been slow, so as not to spook the lawmen, but also because he wasn't sure he wanted to surrender his gun just yet. He didn't know these men, and for all he was aware, they might be in cahoots with Bailey and his partner.

"I said to drop your piece, mister," Fairburn said after a few moments' wait. "Do so now, boy."

Tension rose with the silence, which was finally broken when someone in the crowd yelled, "Those two dead men drew first, Marshal. That there feller shot 'em in self-defense."

Fairburn continued to stare at Law for several more seconds. He could see determination in the man's eyes. What he did not see there was any look of furtiveness, fear, or decadence. "Put your pistols away, boys," he said over his shoulder to his two deputies, who flanked him a few feet to his rear.

"You sure, Al?" one asked.

"I am," Fairburn said. He uncocked his revolver and stuffed it into the holster at his hip. His two deputies followed suit, though to Law it seemed they did so with some reluctance.

"Well, mister?" Fairburn allowed.

Law hesitated only another moment, then eased the hammer down on his Peacemaker and holstered it.

Fairburn and his deputies marched up. "I reckon you ain't about to argue with whoever it was who said you killed these two in self-defense," the marshal said.

"Reckon that would be mighty foolish," Law said with no hint of a smile. "Seeing as how it's the truth."

"You mind tellin' me just what went on here?"

Before Law could respond, an anxious Sara Jane hurried

up and stopped next to the two men. "You all right, John Thomas?" she asked.

The bounty man nodded.

"Mrs. Gibbons," Fairburn said by way of greeting. He was surprised. "Do you know this man?"

"Yes, Marshal, I do. He's an old friend from my home-place." She looked at Law with what he took to be undis-guised affection. "He came here to . . ."

Law shook his head almost imperceptibly.

". . . on some business," Sara Jane corrected herself. "When he learned that I lived in St. Joe, he stopped by to visit." She gave Law another glance, and was reassured. "Then, when he heard about Oliver, he offered to stay around a few days to see if he could be of any help."

Fairburn nodded and looked at Law. "So, what hap-pened here, mister . . . Mister what?"

"J.T. will suffice, Marshal," Law said blandly.

A look of modest annoyance drifted across Fairburn's face, but vanished quickly. "All right . . . J.T. . . . what happened?"

As Law explained the events, he noticed Milt Dalrym-ple and Ned Rogers as well as a couple of other men Law assumed were Pinkerton agents in the crowd. The men were watching him, though they were not close enough to hear anything he or Marshal Fairburn were saying.

When Law finished, Fairburn said, "It all sounds fairly preposterous to me, Mister . . . J.T.," Fairburn said skeptically.

"Why is that, Marshal?" Sara Jane interjected. "I think Mister L . . . John Thomas did quite a wonderful thing." She managed not to blush.

Fairburn almost smiled. "That's no doubt true, ma'am," he said, still trying not to let his humor break forth and also trying not to look at Law. "But there is the question of why these men would've contemplated trying to grab your person here in the midst of a busy mornin' right in the middle of Main Street." He did finally look at Law. "You have any notions on that, mister?"

"Well, I ain't had much time to cogitate on it, of course," Law allowed, "but I did wonder about that when I became aware of what they were plannin'."

"And?" Fairburn asked in exasperation.

"And," Law drawled, "I don't think they were plannin' to actually snatch her right off the street here, Marshal. That'd raise all kinds of stink with you and the Pinkertons. They might not've been the brightest fellahs to tread the fine streets of St. Joe, but they weren't foolish enough to pull a half-witted stunt like that."

"So, what was their plan?" Fairburn pressed.

"I can't know for sure, of course, Marshal," Law continued slowly, still formulating the idea in his mind. "But I think that when they saw Sara . . . Mrs. Gibbons . . . they thought they might gain some favor with their boss by . . ."

"Who is—was—their boss?" Fairburn interrupted.

"That one there," Law said, pointing to Bailey, "lived long enough to say he rode with Tom Ellsworth. I . . ."

Sara Jane gasped, and Fairburn's eyebrows shot up.

Fairburn stroked one long dangling end of his mustache, thinking that over, then suddenly asked, "Why would that feller tell you such a thing, though? About him ridin' with Ellsworth, I mean."

Law shrugged. "I got no idea," Law lied easily. "Maybe his brain was addled from the pain of his wounds."

Fairburn looked dubious, but accepted it for the time being. "Go on, then, with this theory of yours."

"As I was sayin', I think these half-wits saw Mrs. Gibbons, realized who she was, and quickly came up with this cockamamie idea to take her. I expect they were going to try to 'persuade' her to go along with them. Either with a quiet threat—or maybe by tellin' her that they had some news of her husband. With that, she would've gone along willingly with them. Or, I reckon they would have thought."

"That makes some sense," Fairburn admitted.

"It makes perfect sense," Sara Jane insisted.

"Where were you in all this, J.T.?" Fairburn asked. He felt duty-bound to get all the facts.

"I was standin' back out of the way, watchin' over things when those two walked in. Soon as they saw Mrs. Gibbons, they jawed between themselves a few minutes, then left."

"And that's when you went out after them?"

"Yep."

Fairburn stroked the mustache again, then nodded. "Seems like it was self-defense," he acknowledged. "Where're you stayin', should I find reason to ask you a few more questions?"

"You need to talk to me, you contact Mrs. Gibbons," Law said flatly. "She'll get word to me." His tone let it be known that this was not open to question, nor was anyone to think poorly of Sara Jane.

Fairburn glowered a moment, then nodded. He knew Sara Jane, and knew she would not do anything untoward.

"One more thing, Marshal," Law said. "I can't be sure, of course, but I reckon these boys have rewards on 'em, though I expect it'd be mighty small."

Fairburn battled back his disappointment. He, too, had figured that, and was planning on he and his deputies pocketing that money. "You a bounty man?" he asked, trying to mask his annoyance.

"None of your concern, Marshal," Law said flatly.

"Reckon it ain't." Fairburn wasn't sure what he thought about this big, broad-shouldered man. He could be mighty irritating, the marshal had found out already, but he had an air of rightness about him, too. "I'll check into the rewards—if there are any. Come by and see me tomorrow about it."

Law nodded. "Marshal," he said by way of good-bye, touching the brim of his hat. He took Sara Jane's arm and escorted her back into the store.

CHAPTER 10

As HE RODE Toby toward Main Street in the quickly gathering dusk, Law felt odd about leaving Sara Jane in the house alone with Billy Tyler, though he wasn't sure why. He could trust both of them implicitly. Besides, he had no hold on Sara Jane. He finally convinced himself that it was because people might talk; he would never convince himself it was jealousy and desire to have Sara Jane back.

And it had to be done. There were places he needed to go to talk with people where Tyler would not have been at all comfortable. The young Texas Ranger was still too much of a lawman—and a decent person—to make his way easily among some of the saloons Law might have to frequent if he was to pick up any information about either Oliver Gibbons or the outlaws who had escaped. Law also figured that most hardcases, the ones who had been on the wrong side of the law for a good portion of their lives, would pick Tyler out as a lawman right off.

And he needed to get what information he could. It was

imperative to find out if Ellsworth was up to anything—
whether planning to come against him for killing his
cronies or go against Sara Jane. Law also hoped to get a fix
on what had happened to Oliver Gibbons. Sara Jane deserved to know, one way or the other. No one might know
anything—or, more likely, anyone who knew anything
likely wouldn't be talking—but he had to try to find out.

After the incident outside the Bzovys' store the day before, Law, Tyler, and Sara Jane had spent several hours dis-
cussing this—and what to do under various possible
outcomes, as well as trying to come up with plans for keeping the Gibbons family safe. They came to no definite conclusions, because the information they had was so sparse,
but it was decided that Law would make every effort to
learn whatever he could about Ellsworth and what had happened to Gibbons.

After dark had fallen—and after the children were
asleep—Law and Tyler had gone into the barn to make
things look good for any prying eyes. But after waiting an
hour, Law had slipped back into the house. Sara Jane had
left him a quilt, a wool blanket, and a soft pillow in the sitting room. He stretched out on the floor near the stove after
taking a quick check of the house, and was asleep within
seconds.

Law woke before dawn. Stretching in the cold morning
air, he stoked up the parlor stove, made a survey of the
house to make sure all was secure, stoked up the cookstove, put some coffee on, and slipped back outside to the
barn. After daylight, he and Tyler strode to the house and a
filling breakfast of biscuits and gravy, sausages, eggs, and
plenty of hot, heavily sweetened black coffee.

Law and Tyler took turns watching the house and split-
ting firewood out in the backyard before Law sent his
friend to Bzovys' to get himself a winter coat and a pair of

gloves. Tyler came back wearing a thick wool, full-length coat, his .44 Remingtons strapped outside it. He seemed quite pleased with it.

After a fine supper of a thick beef stew and biscuits, Law saddled Toby and began the short ride to the business district on Main Street. The weather had turned even colder, and a light snow had begun to fall. During the short ride, Law decided that he, too, needed something more than his regular frock coat to combat the elements. He stopped at Bzovys', where he finally settled on a charcoal gray caped greatcoat of duck cloth with a wool lining. It buttoned from neck to waist, making it difficult to get at the small Peacemaker in the shoulder holster, but allowing him free access to the big revolver at his waist. Because of his size, the ever-helpful Marge Bzovy arranged to have some alterations made to the garment. While he was there, Law bought two pairs of gloves—one of fur-lined leather, another of wool. He cut most of the fingers off of the latter pair. Wearing those, and still wearing his frock coat, he headed out of the store and rode the short distance to the first bar he found, a dive called the Black Dog.

Tossing his hat on a table, he took a seat with his back to the rear corner, giving him a view of the entire small room. The place was decrepit, the walls, ceiling, sawdust-covered floor, and even the bar itself pocked with bullet holes.

A surly man in a shirt that had long ago been white strolled over and growled, "Whaddaya want, mister?"

"Some goddamn manners'd be a nice start," Law said sarcastically.

The man seemed not to hear. "Whiskey or beer?" he asked.

"Beer," Law said flatly.

The man did not return. Instead, a working girl arrived

with two mugs of beer that had so much foam as to almost have no actual beer. She set the glasses down and dragged a chair closer to Law. She plopped down into it. "My name's Bessie," she said. "I thought you might like some company."

She was a fairly tall, very skinny woman with not much of a discernible bosom despite the low-cut dress she wore. Stringy hair framed a pale, pinched face dominated by large, mostly bloodshot brown eyes. When she smiled, such as it was, her thin lips peeled back to reveal a slew of gaps where teeth should be.

Even if Law had been interested in a woman—other than Sara Jane, of course, even though she was off limits and he accepted that—this would not be the one. However, he was not one for hurting someone unnecessarily, presenting him with something of a quandary. Deciding there would be no easy way to turn her down, he said simply, "Reckon not."

At her crestfallen look, which he had expected, he added, "Leastways not in the back room. But I'd be pleased to have your company here for a spell." He reached into an outer coat pocket, pulled out a very small sheaf of greenbacks, peeled a five-dollar bill off and stuffed it into what little cleavage she had.

Bessie pulled it out, looked at it, and stuffed it back. "That'd buy you a couple of nights," she said in a voice that reminded Law of a train's wheels squealing to an emergency stop.

Law slid a silver dollar across the table to her. "That's for the bartender or whoever else runs the business," he said.

"Thank you," Bessie said shyly.

Law lifted his beer and sort of saluted her. She returned it, and they both took a sip.

"You know anything about those boys who escaped the jail the other day?" Law asked.

Bessie shrugged. "Tom Ellsworth and his cronies? Don't know a whole lot. They never did come in the Black Dog much. We ain't high class enough for 'em, I reckon."

Law had never met Ellsworth or any of the others, but judging by the two men he had killed who had ridden with Ellsworth, he could not picture any of them as being in any way high class. On the other hand, the Black Dog seemed to be the lowest of the low as far as saloons went, and he expected that Ellsworth's men preferred a slightly better establishment.

"Who're the others who escaped with him?" Law asked.

Bessie took a sip of beer. She stared off into space, and Law assumed she was thinking. "Um . . . Matt Meekins, Bart something . . . um, Ragsdale, Charlie Quinlan, and Dan Fou-something." Her brow scrunched up in thought. "Fouquette. That's it."

"They must be some hardcases," Law allowed, taking a gulp of beer. It was warm and what it surrendered in blandness it more than gave up in lack of flavor.

"Yep." Bessie drank some beer and didn't appear to like its taste any more than Law had. "'Course, that's to be expected. After all, they was all sentenced to hang."

"You seen any of them since they broke out of that jail?"

"Nope." Her wide eyes hid no secrets that Law could see. She took another drink of the wretched beer and winced. "This stuff is awful," she muttered.

"That's a fact, ma'am," Law said. He reconsidered the new mouthful he was about to take and left the glass sitting on the table.

"Why're you so interested in those boys?" Bessie asked.

"Well," Law said slowly, "since I sent a couple of Ellsworth's pukes to the boneyard yesterday, I reckon Ellsworth might not be too happy with me. I figure the more

I can learn about 'em, the better prepared I'll be if they decide to try something."

Bessie shrugged.

"Any of his other boys been in here lately?"

"Nope."

"You know what places they might frequent?" Law's voice was even, as he managed to disguise his growing irritation.

"I hear they like the Missouri Belle Saloon a bit down the street on this side, and the Riverside, a bit farther on the other side."

Law nodded. Between Bessie's dull personality, the foul taste of the beer, and the lack of information, he had had his fill of the Black Dog. It was time to try his luck elsewhere. He rose and picked up his hat. "Well, Miz Bessie," he said easily, "it's been right pleasurable bein' in your company, but I best be moseyin' on."

Bessie was a little upset that this tall, handsome, rugged man was snubbing her, but then she remembered the five dollars tucked in her minuscule bosom and she felt better. She rose and took the silver dollar from the table. "Thank you, mister," she said.

Law touched the brim of his hat and sauntered out, apparently ignoring the riffraff who inhabited the place, but on the alert nonetheless in case someone tried something. No one seemed so inclined.

The air was bitter outside, but it cleared his head and felt bracing—for a few moments, anyway. He scratched Toby's forehead and slipped the buckskin a lump of sugar from the several he kept in a coat pocket. He climbed into the saddle and rode slowly down the street, stopping and alighting in front of the Missouri Belle Saloon. It was the closer of the two, and he figured he might as well stop there first.

While it wasn't the finest place he had ever been in, it was several steps up from the Black Dog. A mahogany

bar ran most of the length along the left side. Three bartenders worked behind it. The rest of the long, fairly nar-
row room was occupied by regular tables, faro tables, and
poker tables. Along the back wall was a staircase leading
to the second floor, which was lined by rooms on the back
and two sides. There was a considerable crowd, which
made the inside considerably warmer than outside, and
candle-spiked chandeliers threw plenty of light around
the room.

Law attracted little attention—except from the working
women, most of whom figured this was one man they
might not mind striking up a deal with—as he strode to the
far end of the bar under the second-floor walkway. He
stood so that his back was toward the rear wall and ordered
a shot of whiskey and a beer.

A portly, rather jovial barkeep served the drinks.

"Right busy tonight," Law said.

"Not too bad," the man said.

"You seen Tom Ellsworth or any of his boys lately?"
Law asked bluntly.

"Don't know who the hell you're talkin' about, mister."
The bartender suddenly became defensive and his eyes
darkened with suspicion.

Law's glare let him know he figured the man was lying,
but he said nothing. Just lifted his shot glass in a half
salute, then downed the whiskey in one quick jolt. "Fill 'er
up again," he ordered.

The man did so, then left. He muttered something to another bartender, and both stared at him for a moment. He returned the look back until they went back to their business.
He finished the second shot, then sipped at his beer, turning
down the advances of two pleasant looking cyprians. He
considered spending some time with them, mainly because
if anyone knew anything about Ellsworth and his men—or
what had happened to Oliver Gibbons—it would be such

women. But he decided against taking any of them up on their offer. Thoughts of Sara Jane made having a romp with other women unappealing to a large extent right now. And after his experience—if that's what it could be called—with Bessie just a few minutes ago, he wasn't so sure how much he would learn from any of these soiled doves.

As he sipped at his beer, Law's eyes flickered constantly from one man to another scattered around the saloon. He saw no one he recognized, and no one who particularly looked like he would belong to Ellsworth's gang of ruffians.

Deciding this was also a waste of time, at least for now, Law finished his beer and headed outside. He took Toby's reins and walked him down and across the cold, snowy street. He tied the buckskin to the hitching post and went inside the Riverside, closing the doors behind him to shut out the cold, and stopping just inside. It was mighty similar to the Missouri Belle—same long bar against the left wall, though this one sported a fancier back bar; stairway to the second floor, but here it was in the center-rear of the saloon; a few more faro and poker tables; plus two roulette wheels, one to each side of the stairway. The women seemed a little more attractive, too, and Law began to wonder if his determination to stay away from the soiled doves might not be foolish. He pushed that thought away for now. There would be time for that later, should he decide to go ahead with it.

The Riverside was busier than the Missouri Belle, the noise louder, the smoke thicker. Not seeing any empty tables, Law once again went to the end of the bar, where he could keep an eye on things, and ordered a beer. He sipped at it, wondering how he should go about trying to get information here, considering his lack of success so far.

He was still contemplating his situation when a man left one of the poker tables nearby and came to the bar, stopping not far from Law. He ordered a fresh bottle of whiskey and in the few seconds it took for one of the overworked barkeeps to bring it, he glanced at Law and nodded a greeting before turning his head away. Then he look at Law again.

"You're that fellow killed the two outlaws yesterday outside Bzovys' store, ain't you?" he asked.

Law looked the man over. He was fairly nondescript, wore a bland bib-front shirt, and had a shock of hair that had not seen a comb in weeks and a scraggly beard. He was unarmed—or at least had no weapons showing—and Law doubted the man had a hidden gun. He seemed completely nonthreatening.

"I am," Law finally said, voice even.

"Name's Josh Smith," the man said, holding out his hand. When Law shook it, Smith asked, "You up for some poker, mister?" He did not seem to have realized that Law had not reciprocated by giving his name.

Law did not frequent poker tables, but he had played plenty enough to make him well-versed in it. He thought this might be a way to get some information. "Reckon that'd be fine, Mister Smith," he allowed. He picked up his mug of beer and let Smith lead him to a table near the wall.

"This here is Mister . . ." Smith looked at Law. "I never did get your name."

"Just called me J.T.," Law said flatly.

"All right. Boys, J.T. here is the feller killed them hardcases up the street yesterday. He's gonna join us in the game."

Law pointed at the chair that had its back to the wall. "I'd be mighty obliged if you was to let me set there," he said in not unfriendly tones that still left no doubt as to his determination.

The man sitting there looked like he was about to argue, then remembered what Law had done the day before. He nodded and moved. Law took off his hat, dropped it on the table, pulled out some money, and sat.

CHAPTER 11

"THAT WAS REALLY something yesterday, J.T.," Smith said in awed tones, as one of the other men began dealing.

Law wasn't sure whether Smith was really impressed or if he was being sarcastic, but he finally decided it was the former. The man didn't seem to have the capability for sarcasm, or at least about such an event.

"It was necessary," Law said flatly. He wasn't much for talking of such things, but he figured it might be a way into asking questions about Ellsworth and Gibbons.

"What brought it on?" Smith asked.

Law stared at him a moment before looking at his cards. Either Smith was a lunatic or he was guileless.

"Damn, Josh," another man—the one whom Law had asked to change chairs—said, "you ought not to be askin' such questions."

"I'm interested, Bob," Smith said defensively. "Things like that don't happen every day in St. Joe."

"It ain't mannerly," Bob Lyons offered. He was another

slightly pudgy, plain-faced man, whom Law guessed was a shopkeeper of some kind.

"It's all right, Bob," Law said quietly. "I reckon he don't mean much by it." He turned his glance on Smith. "I don't mind talkin' about it some," he lied. He most certainly would rather not talk about it, but if it might gain him some needed information, he would do so. "But you best learn that your pard Bob, here, is right—it usually ain't mannerly to ask such questions of a man. There's many who'd take powerful exception to it."

Smith's eyes grew wide with concern.

"No reason to be fearful, Mister Smith," Law said soothingly. "Just keep it to mind should such an occasion arise again." He looked at the dealer—a real tinhorn-looking fellow with a fancy town coat over a starched white shirt, a string tie, and a colorful silk vest. A derby sat jauntily atop his slicked-back hair. "Two," he said, and tossed two discards away.

Law checked the new cards. He had two pair, tens and fours. Not great but enough to stick around a bit longer. "Those boys was plannin' some deviltry with a woman of my acquaintance, Mister Smith," he said, looking at the man. "I encouraged them to put aside such a foolish notion, but they was havin' none of it."

"You best watch your back, mister," a fourth man at the table said. "From what I hear, those two men were pardners of Tom Ellsworth, a real bad man. Him and a bunch of his cronies was supposed to hang but was broke out of jail a couple of days ago."

Law gave the man a once-over. He, too, looked like a shopkeeper or other townsman, though unlike Smith and Lyons, he had a hard look to his face, as if he had been through his share of danger and hardship. Law nodded, accepting the information, which, of course, he did not need told to him by such a man.

"You heard anything about where this Ellsworth and his men might be since they skedaddled out of the jail, Mister . . . ?"

"McGaffey. Sam McGaffey. And, no, I don't know nothin' about where those boys are."

To Law, McGaffey didn't seemed particularly worried. "It'd be nice to know if they was plannin' on returnin' here," Law prodded, voice measured.

"I reckon that ain't likely," McGaffey said, tossing in his cards. He leaned back and poured himself a drink, which he jolted down. "The law 'round here might not be the best, but with the Pinkertons bein' such a presence in town, I think Ellsworth and his men are gonna keep a far piece from here."

"Reckon you're right," Law allowed. He, too, tossed in his cards as the bet came around to him.

The tinhorn raked in the pot and passed the deck to Lyons on his left. Lyons began dealing a new hand.

"You boys know anything about that judge who disappeared a few weeks ago?" Law asked as he picked up his cards. He let his glance linger only briefly on each of the other four men at the table.

The others—except for the tinhorn—shook their heads.

"I think he skedaddled to California," Lyons said, eliciting a few chuckles. "I heard he got himself a pile of greenbacks from them outlaws somehow, and I figure he's long gone with that money." He paused to pitch a couple of dollars into the pot. "But why he'd leave that woman of his behind don't make no sense." His grin widened. "That gal might not be some young filly, but goddamn, she sure is a fine figure of a woman. Lordy, what I wouldn't like to do with her if I . . ." The words came to an abrupt halt, and Lyons gulped as fear spread across his face at the look Law cast at him. "Um, I mean, he's got to be a damn fool to leave a good woman and his family like that," Lyons mumbled. He wished he were miles away.

Seeing his friend's discomfort, Smith offered, "I think he's just hidin' out somewhere near here." He dropped out of the hand. "I don't believe he got no money from the outlaws. I think they just threatened him when he convicted Ellsworth and his men, so he slipped out of town until—well, at first till they was hanged, I reckon, but now, well, until those boys're caught again."

"That don't make sense," Lyons countered, wanting to make Law forget the insensitive and untimely comments he had made moments ago. "I think he's gotten himself as far away from these parts as he can. Maybe he's even gone to some far-off place like Europe."

"Nah, Bob," Smith countered. "Like you said, he wouldn't leave his family." He ignored the wince Lyons cast his way at those words, worried that they might anger Law. "I'd wager he's hidin' out close by." He thought a minute as the tinhorn pulled in another pot, and Smith took the cards. He started dealing. "I think he's hidin' in St. Joe, maybe right in his own house."

That raised a chuckle around the table from all but the tinhorn and Law. The bounty man glanced at the gambler, who was neatly stacking his money, seemingly paying little attention to anything being said at the table.

"Ain't likely," McGaffey said somberly. "I think that son of a gun is dead."

"Nah, that can't be," Smith argued. "Somebody would've found him by now. Or we would've heard something. Ain't every day a judge gets killed, ya know."

"Might be," McGaffey allowed.

The men quieted for a little as they studied their cards and placed bets. The tinhorn won the next three pots and looked like he was about to win another when he again was the dealer. Law had been watching him and figured the man was cheating. He did not want to interrupt the flow of talk—if there was to be any more—despite the likelihood that he would not learn anything of value. But he was not about to continue losing money to this card sharp. Law just wanted to warn him with a look that let him know what was going on, but the man refused to look at him. And had said nothing other than curt phrases pertaining to the play of the game.

"You've had yourself a purty lucky run here, bub," Law said as the gambler pulled in another pot.

"Reckon so," the tinhorn said, still not looking at Law.

With his left hand, Law surreptitiously unbuttoned the top button of his frock coat—the only one that was fastened—and pushed the garment open a little, exposing the walnut grip of the small Colt Peacemaker. "I reckon it can't go on forever," he said.

Something about Law's tone made the tinhorn pause in pulling the money toward him. He finally glanced up. While he wouldn't look Law directly in the eyes, he did see enough of the bounty man's face to know that he was treading on dangerous ground here. His quick eyes also took note of the revolver that was now visible. He said nothing, nor even indicated that he understood the implicit warning, but Law was certain he had gotten the message.

The others at the table were aware of the tension, but they were not sure what it was about.

"You know what I think," McGaffey suddenly said into the void. "I think the law's got that judge feller hid somewhere."

"That's mad," Smith said as cards were dealt. "Why would the law do such a thing?"

McGaffey shrugged. "Maybe not the real law, but those damned Pinkertons. Hell, those bastards wouldn't need a reason. It's just the kind of thing they'd do."

Law was interested in that theory a bit more than the

others that had been voiced. But he soon decided it made
no sense. He suspected that McGaffey had just made the
suggestion because he wanted to break the tension that had
formed—and because he probably had some kind of bone
to pick with the Pinkertons. He wasn't the only one, Law
thought with a touch of inner humor.

Thirty minutes later, Law had won two small pots, as
had everyone else except the tinhorn. Law had not learned
anything worthwhile about Ellsworth or Gibbons, and he
decided he probably would not. He gathered up his money,
slapped his hat on, and rose.

"You three boys," he said as Smith, Lyons, and Mc-
Gaffey looked up at him, "might want to find yourselves a
different fellah to sit in with you besides him." He nodded
toward the tinhorn.

"But why . . . ?" Smith started.

McGaffey cut him off. "Why do you think, Josh," he
snapped. "I reckon we really can't trust this dude."

The tinhorn glanced around, suddenly nervous. While
he carried a small derringer in his pocket and these other
men were unarmed, he did not want to risk arrest. He began picking up his money. "Reckon I better be on my way,
too, gentlemen," he offered. He hurried away from the
table while Law was still sanding there.

Law checked his pocket watch, savoring for a moment
the picture of Sara Jane inside the cover. He decided he had
had enough of trying to gain information for one night. He
went out into the cold air. The snow was still coming down,
but not in any large amount, and that was being whipped
about by a bitter wind. He rode back to Sara Jane's, tended
to Toby in the barn, and then went into the house, where he
told Tyler and Sara Jane what he had heard. He again spent
the night on the sitting room floor.

In the morning, Law rode Toby to the Bzovys' store and

got his coat. He tried it on in the store and was pleased with the work the seamstress had done. He paid for the garment—and the work—put it on, and stepped outside. He tied his frock coat to the back of his saddle and rode to Marshal Al Fairburn's office.

"Mornin', J.T.," Fairburn said with a decided lack of enthusiasm. He was still not sure how he felt about this man.

"Marshal." Law sat across the desk from Fairburn.

"Looks like you was right," the marshal said. "Both men had bounty money on 'em, but wasn't much—a hundred bucks apiece."

"Better'n a poke in the eye," Law allowed. He took the pen Fairburn handed him and dipped the nib into the inkwell. He hesitated a moment, regretting that he had insisted on getting this bounty money. He did not like the idea of having his full name on any papers in this area. Then he shrugged and signed, scrawling his name so it was mostly illegible. After counting his money, he asked, "You heard anything about Ellsworth and his boys?"

"Not a peep. I reckon they've lit out."

"You don't really believe that, do you?" Law questioned, his tone sharp.

"Reckon not. I expect they're lookin' for Judge Gibbons—or will want to keep an eye on his wife to see if he contacts her, so I doubt they've gone far."

"What do you think's happened to Gibbons?"

Fairburn stroked the long, dangling ends of his mustache while he thought. "I ain't sure, J.T.," he finally said slowly. "At first I figured he was dead, but now I ain't so sure. In fact, I'm figurin' he's alive. If he was dead, why would those men try to accost Mrs. Gibbons yesterday?"

"Could be that they killed him but are keepin' an eye on Sara . . . Mrs. Gibbons . . . because they think she either might have the money or know where he hid it."

"Reckon that's true," Fairburn said thoughtfully.

"Can you tell me anything about Ellsworth and his men?" Law asked.

"Mean bunch of bastards, as you might expect. Robbed a passel of banks, as well as trains. Have rustled cattle and horses when the opportunity's come up. Robbed stages, killed Lord knows how many unfortunate people. They earned the hangin's they were sentenced to for certain."

"What's the reward on 'em now?" Law asked.

Fairburn stared at him a moment, then queried, "I asked you this before, Mister . . ." he looked down at the paper Law had just signed but could not read the name, ". . . whatever the hell your name is . . . are you a bounty man?" He was not particularly fond of such men, but he wasn't entirely against them, either. Not like some others were. He figured most of them earned their blood money, and he'd rather see someone like Law chasing down bad men like Ellsworth's gang than have to do it himself, putting his deputies in danger.

"And I told you before, that's none of your concern," Law said flatly.

"The hell it ain't," Fairburn snapped. "You're in my jurisdiction, my town, and as the law here in St. Joe, I deserve an answer."

Law wondered how much he should tell the marshal. With warrants out for his arrest in Missouri, like as not, he did not want any lawman knowing too much about him or his past. But he was a pretty good judge of character most times, and he instinctually felt he could trust Fairburn, though he was not yet sure how much.

"I've done some," he allowed. "Enough to know I'm good at it."

"And is that why you're plannin' to go agin Tom Ellsworth and the others?" Fairburn demanded.

"I ain't plannin' on going out lookin' for 'em," Law said.

"But I will take 'em out any way I can should they come after Sara Jane. I do that, I'll want the bounty on 'em. Somebody else gets 'em and thus removes the danger from Sara Jane and her family, they can have the money."

Fairburn's eyes never left Law's. Then he nodded. He wasn't sure why, but he believed Law, and his trust for the man rose.

When he left the marshal's office and was riding back toward the Gibbons house, Law felt as if he were being followed. He tried to check surreptitiously a couple of times but saw no one who seemed to be tailing him. Still, when he got back to the house, he let Tyler know his suspicions and warned him to be even more alert.

He had the same feeling late that afternoon as he headed back for the Riverside, then the Missouri Belle. At the former, he thought he spotted someone showing an interest in him from across the room. At the latter, he became sure. He kept away from people for the most part, watching the man watching him, and keeping his ears open in hopes he would learn something worthwhile about either Ellsworth or Gibbons.

Finally he headed out into the cold night. He mounted Toby and headed slowly up the street. He turned suddenly onto Fourth Street, stopped, and slid out of the saddle. He pushed Toby out of the way, up against the side of the hardware store, and pulled on his leather gloves. Then he waited.

A minute later, the man Law had seen at both saloons turned his horse onto dimly lit Fourth Street.

CHAPTER 12

LAW STEPPED OUT of the shadows as the man rode in front of him. He reached up and latched both hands onto the front of the man's canvas coat and jerked him down from the horse. The spooked animal galloped off down the street.

Law swung the man around and slammed his back hard up against the wood building, then rammed a strong right first into his stomach. The blow had little impact through the heavy garment. Law pasted him twice, then a third time in the face, breaking his nose and, Law thought, one of the man's cheekbones.

The man groaned and sagged. He would have fallen had Law still not had a grip with his left hand on the man's coat, holding him up.

"What's your name, bub?" Law demanded.

"William. William Iverson," the man gasped.

"What're you followin' me for, boy?" Law asked, voice harsh.

"Detective Dalrymple told me to keep a watch on you so . . ."

"You're a Pinkerton?"

"Yessir." Iverson tried to draw himself up, but the pain in his face was still potent, and he leaned back against the building again.

Law suddenly began pounding Iverson all about the body, and even the winter coat could not for long fend off damage. Before long, Iverson, who feebly tried to fight back, began to groan, as ribs cracked and contusions began to grow on his body.

Finally the beating stopped, and Law let Iverson slide down the wall until he was sitting on the cold ground. Law knelt in front of him. "Dalrymple, that dumb puke, was warned what would happen if any of you Pinkerton bastards tried to accost me or anyone connected with Mrs. Gibbons. He should've listened."

Iverson let out another groan, but said nothing.

"It's a plumb pity you've had to pay for his arrogance and stupidity, bub," Law said without sympathy.

Iverson moaned again.

"You're a goddamn lucky son of a bitch, Mister Iverson," Law growled.

"How so?" the Pinkerton managed.

"Because I'm such an even-tempered fellah. Was I ill-tempered, you'd be a goddamn goner now. So you go on back to Dalrymple and tell him to keep his distance from me and anybody I know." He grabbed Iverson's revolver from the hip holster outside the coat and emptied it. "You got another piece on you, boy?" he asked.

Iverson shook his head, and moaned when that produced all kinds of pains.

"Good." Law shoved the pistol into the front of Iverson's coat, and rose. "Best remember what I said, and tell your boss that should he be stupid enough to send another man to follow me, I'll kill that cuss—and then come for him."

Law mounted Toby and rode off into the night, leaving Iverson on the cold ground. He did not really care much if Iverson froze to death there.

LAW SPENT THE next two nights haunting St. Joseph saloons, trying to get information. Most of the time was spent in either the Missouri Belle or the Riverside. He spoke little and asked few questions, though he would do so when an opportunity presented itself, when someone else happened to mention something that touched on one of the subjects in which Law was interested. Mostly, though, he listened intently to conversations around him. He sat in on poker and faro games on occasion in his quest.

It was frustrating in many ways. He heard plenty about how bad Ellsworth and his gang were, but nothing solid about where they might be or what they were up to. Nor was he able to learn anything about what had happened to Gibbons or where the judge could be if the outlaws had not found him.

He did, however, decide that spending some intimate time with some of the women working the saloons might be in order to try to get information. He felt extremely odd about doing so, though. He had, of course, no real claim to Sara Jane, but spending time with any other woman right now seemed to him to be somehow violating Sara Jane. He knew that was foolish—after all, he hadn't seen her in well over a decade, she was married, her husband still might return, and she had a passel of children—but the feeling remained.

Still, even that provided no information, and after two fruitless, though fairly exciting, episodes, he gave up the notion of trying to find out anything that way.

But with the talk he overheard in the saloons, he did begin to believe that Gibbons was dead. There had been no word from him, and Sara Jane fully believed that her husband would, somehow, when he thought he could do so without endangering himself or his family, find a way to get word to her. He might not want to tell her where he was because he was afraid for his safety or that of his family, but he would contact her somehow. And Sara Jane believed he still would, very soon, probably right after Ellsworth's gang was brought to heel again.

There were other times, however, that Law thought that perhaps he just wanted to believe Gibbons was dead. If that were the case, Law fully intended to try striking up his romance with Sara Jane again. He even thought it would be acceptable to her—after a decent period of mourning, of course.

Law stopped in at Marshal Fairburn's every day to see if the lawman had heard anything. On one of his visits, a frustrated Law said, "Why don't you have one of your deputies ride on out to some of the farms in the area and ask if any of those folks have seen any strangers around of late? Might be that Gibbons is hidin' out in such a place. Or that Ellsworth has been by, maybe lookin' for some supplies or somethin'."

"Reckon I might could do that," Fairburn acknowledged. He grinned at the surprise Law showed at the use of the Texas expression. Then he nodded. "I'm from Nacogdoches," the marshal said. "Fought for the Cause but found the old homeplace not much to my likin' afterward, what with all them goddamn Yankee carpetbaggers. I went lookin' for a new place to hang my hat, and found out things wasn't so bad 'round these parts."

Law nodded, his liking for Fairburn increasing.

"As I was sayin'," Fairburn continued, "I might could send both deputies out, shortenin' the time it took to do this checkin'."

"That'd be good," Law allowed.

"'Cept that it'd leave me with no deputies. Now, if I was to have a stand-in deputy . . ." He did not need to finish.

"No thanks, Marshal," Law said. "There's reasons that'd not be a very good notion, though I can't rightly explain what they are."

Fairburn nodded. He had expected that reaction. And even suspected why it would be given. "Well, then, I reckon I can send only one at a time."

"I wish it could be different, Marshal," Law said with a touch of regret in his voice. He paused, then added, "Something else you might consider is sendin' wires to nearby towns or places you think either Ellsworth's gang or Gibbons might've gone off to."

"Either of 'em might've tried to get lost in a big city like Kansas City or St. Louis," Fairburn mused. He nodded. "I'll do that, too."

But neither of those actions produced any more credible results than the time Law had spent in saloons.

"Deputy O'Connor thought he might have somethin' at a farm six, seven miles northeast of town, but it turns out the stranger that come by was just some saddle tramp."

Law shook his head. "Damn," he muttered. He had thought something might turn up from these activities.

"I ain't too surprised. Like the James boys, Ellsworth has a passel of friends and family in these parts," Fairburn said sourly. As a former Reb, he had some sympathy for the Jameses and Ellsworth. But as a lawman, he could not let any sympathy get in the way of doing his job. Besides, he often thought, most men would have changed their ways after all these years.

"So they could be stayin' nearby, being sheltered by kinfolk or friends," Law said more than asked.

"Yep."

"It's lookin' more and more like Gibbons is dead," Law said. "It don't seem likely that nobody's seen him."

"Good chance one of Ellsworth's kinfolk did see him and got word to that scurrilous cuss."

Law nodded. He was torn. Again, he thought that if Gibbons could be proved to be dead, he could court Sara Jane again; but he knew she loved—or at least had loved—her husband and would miss him if he were dead. And he would not want her to be in pain.

"I suppose it's possible that Ellsworth's left these parts for good, figurin' that since he was sentenced to hang, even family and friends might not be enough to keep him from the noose," Fairburn said hopefully.

"That'd be damned good," Law said. "But I'd feel a sight better if we knew for certain."

"So would I, J.T., so would I."

A discouraged Law headed back to the Riverside that night. He knew by now that he would almost certainly not learn anything that would help him deal with the situation. That was extremely disheartening. Law was used to simply tracking down some gang of hardcases and taking care of business. To not know who he was up against, really, or where they were, or even if they were in the vicinity, was galling.

He unbuttoned his greatcoat and strolled toward the far end of the bar. He did not see the furtive-looking man who scurried out the front doors as soon as he had spotted Law.

At the very corner of the bar, he stopped. He had given up trying to be friendly to the bartenders here, so he simply ordered a beer and dropped his hat on the bar. He surveyed the room.

The place was pretty full, with most of the tables occupied and all three faro tables busy. The working girls were taking a steady stream of men up the stairs nearby. The noise was considerable and the smoke thick throughout the place. Just to his left, one of the two roulette wheels clacked regularly, accompanied by the rare cheers of the winners and the much more frequent groans of the losers.

When his beer came, Law took a long draught of it before setting the glass down. He pulled off the greatcoat and laid it on the bar next to his hat. With so many people and the plethora of lanterns and candle chandeliers, it was plenty warm in the Riverside.

Law lit a thin cigar and puffed away, sipping beer between releasing streamers of smoke to join the cloud that hovered over the room. He continued just watching the crowd, trying to decide whether it would be worth his while to join one of the poker games. Faro was out of the question, in part because all three tables along the left wall from where he stood allowed only the dealer to sit with his back to the wall, but also because he thought that bucking the tiger was a damn fool thing to do.

He instantly grew more alert when the saloon doors opened and four men walked in. Law could not see them clearly but three of them had a demeanor that even from this distance signaled trouble. The fourth was a ferrety-looking little man, whose hands and eyes darted nervously as he spoke to the other three. He pointed in Law's direction, then scooted behind the other three, who began striding toward Law.

The bounty man kept his left hand on the glass of beer, stuck the cigar in his teeth, then dropped his right hand down and eased out his Peacemaker. He set the revolver on its side on the bar, hand resting lightly on it. The weapon was hidden behind his coat. He oozed calmness as he took stock of the men approaching him. All were about five-foot-ten and all three had thick beards and mustaches. Two wore canvas dusters, which they swept back away from the pistols at their hips. The other was clad in a thigh-length wool rancher's coat, his two pistols strapped outside the garment. The man on the left as Law watched them had his hat hanging on his back, held by a thong around his neck. The other two wore battered, dull-colored, tall-crowned hats. As they grew closer, Law could see the hard look in their eyes, even through the smoke. All in all, they had the appearance of men who were used to danger—and used to killing.

They stopped maybe ten feet from Law. Several men at the bar nearby scooted out of the way, a couple of them heading for the door, the others moving to where they could watch while being—they hoped—out of the line of fire, if that's what it came to.

"You been askin' a heap of questions 'bout things that don't really concern you, pard," the one without the hat said.

Law said nothing, just stared at the three men with an expressionless face.

"There's some don't take kindly to such," Hatless continued, seemingly just the tiniest bit annoyed at the lack of reaction on Law's part.

"That so?" Law finally said around the thin cigar. He noted that the man doing the talking had two pistols stuck into a sash, butts facing forward, barely visible under the duster.

"That's right. It's a bad habit, especially when your snoopin' causes trouble for friends of ours, like them two boys you killed down the street yonder a few days ago."

"They were assholes," Law allowed.

The three men's eyes widened in surprise, then narrowed to slits in anger. "Reckon you're one of those knob-headed sons of bitches needs to be taught a lesson."

Law smiled insolently. He was vaguely aware that the noise level in the saloon had dropped to something approaching silence. "Not from the likes of a puke like you," Law said softly. He cocked the hammer on the Colt without seeming to move. "Now go away, before y'all get yourselves hurt. Or worse."

CHAPTER 13

THE THREE MEN seemed to move at the same instant. With the easiest access to his pistols, the man with the short coat managed to draw first, yanking out one of his two guns.

Law tossed his beer glass at the other two men with his left hand. With his right, he snapped his already cocked Colt up and fired once, drilling the man in the short coat through the forehead.

The man staggered back a few steps, dead but not yet knowing it. He finally crumpled.

Law did not see him fall. He had swung toward the other two men. He was a little surprised to see that Hatless had so swiftly drawn his two pistols. The man fired twice. One bullet thudded into the wall behind Law, while the other tore through his short collar, searing his neck a little. He winced involuntarily, then snapped off two shots at Hatless.

But the man was moving, ducking and backing away, and both lead bullets missed him.

"Dammit," Law snapped fiercely, though not loudly. He

fired again, hitting the third man, who had been struggling to get his pistols out. One had gotten snagged inside his duster, and in fighting to free it, he had moved a few feet to his right, directly into the path of Law's bullet.

As his partner fell, Hatless fired twice more at Law, both bullets grazing Law's right side, along the ribs.

Law hissed with the sharp burn but did not flinch. He fired, hitting Hatless in the chest.

Hatless fell backward, landing on a table and bouncing off it. He hit the floor and rolled, trying to raise his pistol. He knew he was going to die, and he wanted to get one more shot off in hopes of taking his opponent with him.

Law stepped out from behind the corner of the bar and strode toward Hatless. The wounded man managed to bring one of his pistols to bear, though his arm was wavering.

"Don't," Law warned.

"Go to hell, mister," Hatless responded. He continued raising the weapon and tried to squeeze the trigger.

Law shot him in the head. He swung around, seeing the furtive little man who had pointed him out to the three out-laws heading quickly for the door. Law dropped the big Peacemaker, now empty, into its holster and yanked out the smaller version from his shoulder holster. He fired once, the bullet slamming into the side of the door, inches from the man's head.

The man froze, one hand on the door.

"Next one cracks your skull, bub," Law warned. "Now ease your way back toward me. You make any move I don't like and you'll die of lead poisoning."

The man backed toward him, arms in the air, and stopped when Law told him to do so.

Law shoved the Colt into the shoulder holster. "Turn around," he ordered.

The man did so, displaying a thin, sallow face and wide,

frightened eyes. He was a little man, scrawny, unshaven, dirty. Law changed his opinion of the man—he looked more like a rat than a ferret, as a ferret was often a handsome little animal. There was nothing handsome about this odious little man.

"What're you gonna do with me, mister?" the man asked nervously.

Law suddenly slammed the heel of his hand against the man's forehead, knocking him back several feet before he fell on his behind. Law walked up to him, grabbed his greasy coat, and yanked him to his feet. "Who do you work for, you miserable little bastard?" Law demanded.

"Nobody," the man squeaked.

"You're a lyin' sack of shit, bub," Law snapped. "You pointed me out to them fellahs. I do not take kindly to people who try to set me up for getting shot. Now, who do you work for?"

"They—them three you just killed—passed 'round word yesterday that whoever pointed you out to 'em would get twenty dollar," he squawked. His voice warbled with fear. "When I saw you come in here, I went and found 'em, brought 'em here, and pointed you out. I didn't know they was gonna try causin' you no harm."

"You didn't, did you?" Law said sarcastically, spotting Marshal Al Fairburn and his two deputies hurrying in. "Did you think they were going to come courtin' me, you stupid peckerwood?"

Before the man could say anything else, Fairburn asked, "Who's this, J.T.?"

"Don't know his name, Marshal," Law responded. "But he's the fellah responsible for the deaths of those three damn fools there." He pointed.

Fairburn's eyebrows rose as he spied the carnage. "What happened?" he asked.

With practiced hands, Law quickly reloaded his pistols while he explained it to the lawman.

Fairburn accepted it. He was sure that the three dead men would prove to be connected with Ellsworth, and he had come to trust Law. "What about this one?" he asked, chucking his chin in the rat's direction.

"Well, I don't expect we can hang him," Law drawled. "But I reckon settin' a man up for his murder might could be worth a spell in the penitentiary."

"Sounds sensible to me, J.T." He turned to one of his deputies. "Earl, take this little cuss over to the jail. On the way there, stop by the undertaker's and have Johnson send someone over here to collect these carcasses."

Earl nodded, grabbed the small man by the collar, and dragged him off.

Fairburn saw the blood on Law's neck and side. "You all right, J.T.?" he asked.

"I'm fine," Law said with a shrug. "Just got grazed a couple of times."

"I can have Deputy O'Connor rustle up Doc Vickery for you."

"Ain't necessary, Marshal."

Fairburn nodded. "You know who those men are?" he asked.

"Not their names. But the one over there," he pointed, "who did all the talkin', said I was puttin' my nose in business that didn't concern me. And he said those two I killed the other day down at Bzovys' were friends of theirs. I figure they're with Ellsworth."

"My thoughts, too." He paused. "That might make it even more dangerous for you 'round here, J.T."

"Ellsworth and his scum don't scare me none, Marshal," Law said with a shrug. "And I'm always on my guard."

"Sure you don't want to be a deputy for me?" Fairburn asked with a grin. "You'd make a hell of a lawman."

"I'd like as not cause you more trouble than help, Al," Law chuckled. "You need me for anything else?"

"Reckon not." He paused, then smiled crookedly. "I suppose you'll be wantin' any bounty money on these dumb bastards."

"I do."

"Stop by tomorrow. Hopefully by then I'll know who they are—and how much their carcasses are worth to somebody."

Law nodded and walked back to the end of the bar. There was a full shot glass sitting there next to his coat and hat.

"Compliments of the house, mister," one of the bartenders said.

Law nodded, lifted the drink in a salute to the man, then jolted it back, enjoying the sensation as it burned its way down his gullet. It was good stuff, not the usual rotgut they served. He pulled on his greatcoat and slapped on his hat, then ambled out.

SARA JANE WAS properly horrified when she saw the blood on Law's shirt and heard that he had been in another gunfight, but she calmed down quickly enough when she found that the wounds were superficial. She went about treating them with quiet efficiency.

While she cleaned the wounds and bandaged the two small ones on his ribs, Sara Jane said, "Maybe we should just end this pretense of you spending the nights out in the carriage house."

"That'd like as not set tongues a-waggin'," Law said.

"To the devil with them," Sara Jane said, face flushing bright pink.

"Why Miz Sara Jane," Law said in mock horror, "you just might set me to blushin', here."

Sara Jane turned, snapping hazel eyes toward him. "I'm serious, John Thomas," she said in tones that underlined her words. "I don't give a hoot what people think no more. I'm in danger, my children are in danger, and you've had two gunfights over the situation in less than a week." She shuddered. "Lord almighty, John Thomas, you've killed five men in that time."

"I don't know, Sara Jane," Law said dubiously.

"People here who're my friends aren't going to talk," Sara Jane said firmly. "And those who do wouldn't really be friends, now would they?"

"Reckon not."

"Anybody else who isn't a friend and who talks poorly about me isn't worth frettin' over. And, mind you, there's been no end of such folks already since Oliver disappeared."

"Reckon it can't get much worse then, can it?" Law said more than asked.

"Reckon not."

Law thought it over a few moments, then nodded, wincing as he was reminded that a bullet had creased his neck less than an hour ago. "I reckon Billy there ought to stay out in the barn, though," he added. "He ain't fit for livin' inside a house." After savoring Tyler's and Sara Jane's look of shock for a couple of seconds, he grinned widely, then laughed.

The others joined him.

Used to sleeping on the hard ground, Law and Tyler thought it nearly luxurious to sleep on the sitting room floor with quilts, blankets, and soft, thick pillows.

Late the next morning, Law stopped by Marshal Fairburn's office.

After greeting Law, the marshal said, "While you didn't hit the jackpot with those three fellers, J.T., you did pick up a sight more than you did with those two the other day. Five hundred greenbacks on Lloyd Noonan—he's the one you said did all the talkin'"—and two fifty each on the other two: Burt Furbee and Dewey Nash."

"It'll keep me in beans for a spell," Law allowed. He poured himself some coffee and sat. "You never did tell me what the bounty is on Ellsworth and the pukes who escaped with him."

"And you never told me your full name, J.T.," Fairburn countered.

"It's right there on those papers I signed the other day," Law said, with the hint of a grin.

"That wasn't writin', J.T.," Fairburn said with a snort. "I've seen chickens scratchin' in the barnyard made more legible marks than you did."

Law returned Fairburn's grin. He decided he could trust this marshal with the information. "Law's my name, Al," the bounty man said with another grin. "John Thomas Law."

"Now I'm sure you ought to be one of my deputies," Fairburn said with a chuckle. "Hell, maybe I should be one of your deputies."

"I don't reckon that'd sit very well with the town fathers," Law said dryly.

"Gettin' Ellsworth would be the real jackpot, J.T.," Fairburn said. He rose and got himself some coffee. As he was pouring, he said, "Ellsworth's got five thousand on his head. Matt Meekins is worth twenty-five hundred; the others are worth a thousand each."

"Wouldn't be a bad hunk of change," Law noted. He signed the papers and took the thousand dollars for Noonan, Furbee, and Nash. He stuck it into a pocket of his greatcoat. "How many more men does Ellsworth have?" he asked, as he reached for his enameled coffee cup.

"Other than the men who escaped with him, can't be more than two, three, I'd say," Fairburn said after a few moments' thought, accompanied by mustache-stroking.

"The odds're lookin' better," Law murmured.

"I can't be sure, you understand, but from all we've heard about his gang, he had a dozen or so men ridin' with him. Sometimes there'd be some others who'd throw in with him, but I don't figure they were regular members of his gang. And I don't reckon they'd be in any hurry to get themselves shot up comin' after you or Mrs. Gibbons."

"That's good to know," Law commented dryly.

"It's better'n knowin' there's still a dozen of 'em after you," Fairburn said flatly.

"Reckon that's a fact." Law drained his coffee and walked over to hang the cup on a peg near the stove. "Well, Marshal, I best be on my way."

"Watch your back, J.T.," Fairburn said as he turned back to his paperwork.

THE NEXT COUPLE of days were uneventful. Law didn't even see any Pinkertons trailing him. He spent much of the daylight hours at the house, doing chores with Tyler, trying to keep his mind off of Sara Jane and what she meant to him—and what he would like to be doing with her. He spent the evenings at various saloons, most of the time in either the Riverside or the Missouri Belle, still trying to come up with information on the whereabouts of Tom Ellsworth or Oliver Gibbons.

But it had become even more frustrating. He was something of a celebrity now, and everyone wanted to buy him drinks and occupy his time. He was pleasant enough to everyone, but he grew increasingly irritated. Everyone had his notions about the two men's whereabouts, but no one had any facts.

The bright spot was that there had been no trouble, and he began to think Ellsworth and what men he had left with him were long gone. That got Law to thinking, and on the third night after the shootout at the Riverside, he had made up his mind.

While he, Tyler, and Sara Jane were eating supper at the dining room table and the children were doing so at the table in the kitchen, Law suddenly said, "I reckon it's time you went on back to Texas, Billy."

CHAPTER 14

"HAVE YOU GONE *loco,* J.T.?" Tyler sputtered, almost choking on his chicken pie.

"Nah, Billy," Law said. He felt a touch of sadness at doing this, but he really thought he should push ahead. "I just . . ."

"There's a heap of danger still out there," Tyler said, putting down his fork. "You can't watch over this house all the time by yourself." In his anger and concern, his eccentric expressions had left him. He couldn't help but feel that Law no longer trusted him, though he could think of no reason why.

"And the children will miss him terribly," Sara Jane interjected.

Law had been surprised at first at how well Tyler had taken to the children. It was not unusual to find the lanky Texas Ranger rolling around the floor with the two younger children, laughing just as wildly as they, while the oldest, Lemuel, watched. All three—Lemuel, Janie, and Walter—looked up to Tyler.

"I know they will, Sara Jane," Law said, suddenly feeling put upon. "Hell . . . um, pardon me, Sara Jane . . . heck, I'll miss the old cuss. But I reckon that his folks . . . well, the Rangers back there are missing him something powerful and can make good use of his services. The man has a life to live." He looked at Tyler. "I'm plumb proud that you've come all this way with me. Ain't a man I trust more and would rather ride beside when times get tough . . ."

"Then why the h . . . ? Why send me off?"

Law sighed again. This was not as easy as he thought it was going to be. Maybe he should've put more thought into this before he embarked on it, he wondered. But it was too late for that now.

"Look, Billy, you got important work to do back in Texas. More important than just tendin' to children. Not that there's anything wrong with mindin' young'uns. And I think most of the danger here's passed, that's the important thing."

"You sure?" Tyler asked skeptically.

"Purty certain. I talked with Marshal Fairburn the other day, and from what he says, unless Ellsworth plans to return to St. Joe himself—with those others who broke out of jail with him—he ain't got that many men left. And I don't figure Ellsworth's got any hankerin' to come back here. Not with a five-thousand-dollar price on his head."

Tyler went back to eating while he thought that over. "Truth to tell," he said after a bit, "I am feelin' some like a starvin' tick on a dead dog." When Sara Jane gave him a questioning look, he said, "Useless, ma'am. I'm used to chasin' bad men and such, not sittin' around in a fine house just waitin' for somethin' to happen. I've had a jim-dandy time here horseplayin' with the young'uns and all, but I reckon J.T.'s right—it's time for me to get back to rangerin'."

"I don't know, Mister Tyler," Sara Jane said. "I . . ."

"Mister Tyler now?" Tyler said with a smile. "I decide it's a good idea to head on back to Texas, and you stop callin' me 'Billy'?"

Sara Jane slapped him lightly on the arm. "You stop," she said in mock anger. She sighed. "Are you sure we'll all be safe, John Thomas?" she asked. "I mean, without Billy here keepin' watch over us while you go about your business tryin' to find Oliver."

"Like I said, I don't think Ellsworth or his men will be back here. We'll be all right."

Sara Jane looked at Tyler, who nodded. He did not think it necessary to tell the woman that if any other bad man wanted to make his mark by going against John Thomas Law—or if Ellsworth sent some would-be hardcases after him—they would be taking on a lot more than they bargained for.

"Well, I can't see waitin' now that the decision's made," Tyler said, spirits restored already. He was not a man to be held down by gloom for very long. "I figure to catch the train soon's I can tomorrow." He glanced over at Law. "'Less you need me to be here another day or two, J.T.?"

"Reckon not." He knew that once Tyler had accepted the decision he would be pretty eager to get back. As he had told Sara Jane, Tyler was a man of action. Sitting around not doing much of anything did not sit well with him.

When they were told, the children were, as expected, quite disappointed that Tyler was leaving. They had become attached to him, especially Janie and Walter, the two youngest. Sara Jane had a devil of a time trying to make them understand, but she finally gave up, at least with Walter. Janie grasped it a little after a while. Still, they all went to the train station early the next afternoon to see Tyler off.

By the next day, the children were calm and, while they still missed Tyler, they found other things to occupy their growing minds.

* * *

WITH THE CHILDREN in bed, Law and Sara Jane sat at the kitchen table, sipping coffee and eating a cherry pie she had made that afternoon. Afterward, with a fresh cup of coffee in front of him, Law lit a cigar and leaned back. Sara Jane rose, walked to a cabinet, and pulled out a bottle of whiskey. She returned to the table and poured some into Law's coffee.

"I'm not sure it's any good," she said apologetically. "Oliver's had it settin' there for quite a spell."

"Teetotaler was he?" Despite his own problems with strong liquor some years ago, Law tended to dislike—or maybe it was distrust—men who did not drink at all.

"Not entirely," Sara Jane said, sitting. "But he tended to refrain from strong spirits here in the house."

Law nodded. He wanted so much to dislike Oliver Gibbons, but it was difficult. Except for the purported bribery and subsequent disappearance, he seemed to be a decent fellow. After all, how bad a man could he be if he had married Sara Jane and she loved him?

He blew out a long stream of smoke, then said suddenly, "I think it's time you went back to Texas, too."

"What?" Sara Jane asked, looking at him in surprise. She was even more shocked than she had been when Law had suggested that Tyler should return to Texas.

"You heard me, Sara Jane," Law said quietly.

"Why ever would I do that?" she questioned. "I've spent almost half of my life here, I bore my children here, my life is here." She paused. "And my husband will return here," she added firmly.

"I don't think so, Sara Jane," Law commented, still speaking softly.

"What do you mean?" she snapped.

"There's every chance that your husband is dead, Sara Jane," he said gently.

"No, I don't believe that," she said, tears welling up in her eyes.

"If it's not true, the chances of him returning here are mighty slim, Sara Jane." He wanted to reach out and hold her, but he was sure she would misconstrue it. He also was not sure he could stop himself from going further.

"No," Sara Jane insisted. "He's alive and will come back. Oliver would never abandon his family. He's in hiding somewhere, waiting for it to be safe for him to return and waiting until we are out of danger."

"That's not likely," Law said, holding up his hand, with the cigar between the first two fingers, to forestall any protest. "But even if he is alive and is fixin' to return to you and the young'uns—hell, he'd have to have lost his reason to leave you willingly—movin' back to Texas makes sense."

"But why? I see no reason to . . ."

"Whether he's dead or alive, the danger to you will continue. Even if Ellsworth is caught again—and hanged—the law and the Pinkertons're going to keep lookin' for Oliver, and they'll be watchin' and harassin' you."

"Why? I don't know where he is." Her hands fretted on the table.

"They'll figure that if he is alive, he'll try to contact you sooner or late. It'll get worse, I reckon, if they learn that he's crossed the divide. Or even if they begin to suspect it because he hasn't been spotted in a long spell. If that's the case, they'll harass you even more, thinking that Mister Gibbons must have told you what he did with the money."

"But he didn't," Sara Jane protested. "I've told them that."

"You've seen the way the Pinkertons operate," Law said evenly. "They're not going to believe you, no matter what you say. Which means they'll keep after you."

Sara Jane sat thinking that over, not liking it one little bit, but knowing, deep down, that it was probably true.

"Then there's also the problem posed by Ellsworth and his men."

"I thought you said they'd skedaddled," Sara Jane said, casting a sharp look his way. "It's why you told Mister Tyler to leave."

"I did say that, and I still believe it. But . . . well, things change, Sara Jane. You know that. I expect that for now, they're lookin' hard for Mister Gibbons." It still galled him to say the name. "And they have a mighty lot of friends and kin in these parts, which means they have a lot of eyes. If Mister Gibbons . . ."

"Please, call him Oliver," Sara Jane said.

Law nodded, liking that even less. "If Oliver is hidin' out somewhere not far from here, he's bound to be seen by someone with ties to Ellsworth. And, while it ain't likely, Ellsworth might have a man or two in town keepin' an eye on you to see if Oliver shows up here. If they find him and he has the money on him—or tells them where it is—they'll like as not leave you alone. But they will kill him," he added bluntly. He didn't want to hurt her, but he had to make her understand.

She winced, and the tears continued, but she refused to look away.

"If he doesn't have the money on him and won't tell them where it is, they'll kill him and then come for you. And if they can't find him, sooner or late, they'll come after you for the same reason as the Pinkertons—to see if you know where he is, or where their money is."

Sara Jane didn't know what to say.

"The trouble, Sara Jane," Law went on slowly after another slug of whiskey-laced coffee, "is that I can't be here forever to protect you." He wished he could, and he hoped she could see that in his eyes. The worst thing would be if he stayed around a while, and Gibbons returned. He was not sure he would be able to control his reaction to such a situation.

"You could stay long enough to see the danger past," Sara Jane suggested.

"There ain't no tellin' how long that'd be, Sara Jane," Law said flatly. "A month? Six? A year? Sooner or late, I'm going to have to leave, and when I do, unless the situation is resolved, either the Pinkertons, the law, or Ellsworth's men—or all of 'em—will show up as soon as I'm out of town."

A sinking feeling clutched at Sara Jane's heart.

"Plus I can't stay in this house much longer, either. I know you don't give a hoot that some tongues're already waggin' about these livin' arrangements. It gets much more than another couple of weeks, and your reputation will be sullied here beyond repair. That happens, and Oliver does return, it'll kill him to have to live under those circumstances."

He stubbed out the cigar on the pie plate. "Look at it this way, Sara Jane," he finally continued. "If Oliver has crossed over—or if he gets snuffed out sometime in the near future—you'll be a heap safer in Texas. You'll have your family there. You pa's a rich man and can afford to buy protection. Besides, I'll be around, as will Billy, and even Abe Covington. You'd have a heap of people watchin' out for you and the young'uns."

Sara Jane nodded dully.

"And, if Oliver has skedaddled and has no intent on comin' back, you'll be much better off with your kinfolk in Texas than here with people talkin' and the threat of the Pinkertons or Ellsworth lingerin' on."

"I suppose," Sara Jane sighed. She did not want to think about Oliver dying or being killed. She wanted even less to consider the possibility that he might have abandoned her and the children. That was just too much for her to take. "But what if he's still alive and aims to come back to us as soon as he can?" he asked.

"Maybe he is," Law acknowledged, though he didn't believe it. "If so, there's still a heap of problems to be overcome. He ain't likely to show up as long as Ellsworth is roamin' loose. If those boys get caught and hanged, he might think it's safe enough to come in. But then he'd still have to deal with the local law or the Pinkertons. Maybe this has all been a big misunderstandin', and he'll be able to clear his name when he shows up. If that happens, he won't have no trouble findin' you in Texas. And if you want to move back here after that, well, no one's going to stop you."

Sara Jane nodded, still not convinced.

Law offered a small smile that he hoped might raise her spirits some. "And if he's hidin' out because he did do something wrong, he might feel more free to come lookin' for you in Texas than here, where too many eyes are lookin' for him. He'd have some protection, too, down in Texas, if he followed you there, against both the Pinkertons and Ellsworth."

Sara Jane sat there thinking about it all for a bit.

She looked tired and drawn, but Law thought she was still beautiful, and his heart went out to her. Seeing her hesitation, he said, "I am fixin' to stay here as long as you need to make arrangements, though I'd suggest that not be too long. And, of course, I'll escort you and the children all the way to Austin."

She finally nodded. Worry and reluctance played across her face. "I'll start makin' arrangements first thing," she said in resignation. She cared deeply for this house and would miss it. But she knew, too, that Law was right—there was far more safety in Texas, and her children's safety had to come first.

Law tentatively reached out a hand and lightly clasped one of her forearms. "I know this is hard on you, Sara Jane," he said softly. "But it's best."

"I know," she said, sobbing softly. She stared at him for some moments, and was surprised to see love in his piercing, blue-green eyes. Oliver had never looked at her in quite that way. She felt a burst of reciprocal feeling deep down inside her, which frightened her, though she also enjoyed its warmth.

SARA JANE AND Law went to visit Judge Henry Spellman the next morning, leaving the children in the care of Spellman's wife, Judith, who was Sara Jane's closest friend in St. Joseph.

Fighting back tears the whole time, Sara Jane explained that she had decided it best that she leave the area and return to Texas, at least for the foreseeable future, and she asked Spellman to help her with selling the house and settling her affairs.

"Are you certain you want to do this, Mrs. Gibbons?" Spellman asked nervously, unsettled by the presence of the big, stone-faced Law standing, thumbs casually hooked into his belt, back near the door to the front lobby of his office next to the courthouse.

"No, I don't really want to, Judge," Sara Jane answered truthfully. "But we—I—think it best for me and the children, what with all that's happened of late."

"Is this man coercing you?" Spellman asked. "Forcing you into this decision?" He was afraid, but he was also a man used to wielding power, and he refused to be intimidated.

Sara Jane smiled wanly through the tears. "No, Judge. John Thom . . . John has been a source of strength, allowing me to get through these most difficult times."

Spellman looked at her skeptically, then glanced at the bounty man. He had, of course, heard what Law had done both at Bzovys' store and at the Riverside, and it made him wonder—and worry. Despite the hardness etched on the big man's face and eyes, however, Spellman saw something honorable in Law.

"And you, sir, are you planning to stand by Mrs. Gibbons"—he put ever so little emphasis on the name—"all the way to Texas?" the judge demanded.

"I am," Law replied without hesitation.

Spellman nodded. "I'll help you, Mrs. Gibbons," he said. "Now you go on home and begin your packing or whatever else you need to do. You let me worry about the rest."

"Thank you, Judge," Sara Jane said, rising, making the judge scramble to his feet. She shook his hand.

Law held the door for her and they went through it into the lobby. As he went to open the door to the outside for her, he glanced through the window in the door. He did not like what he saw.

"Stay here, Sara Jane," he ordered. He made sure that his greatcoat was unbuttoned and pushed partially open, allowing him access to his pistols. Then he opened the door and stepped outside, into the face of four cocked pistols and a shotgun.

CHAPTER 15

"WHAT'S GOING ON, John Thomas?" Sara Jane asked, venturing outside, all wide-eyed and fearful, her tears gone.

"Why don't you tell her, Law?" Milt Dalrymple said. He was the only one of the six Pinkertons not aiming a gun at Law. Instead, Dalrymple stood there with a mocking look on his square-jawed face, which was red from the wind and the cold. He looked almost jaunty in his duster—which Law figured he was wearing over his town coat to make himself look more impressive—and his derby. He was holding something over his shoulder, though Law could not tell what it was.

"Go on back inside, Sara Jane," Law commanded. He was in a deep spot of trouble here and was calculating how many of these Pinkertons he could get before one of them sent a fatal bullet into him, and he did not need Sara Jane in the line of fire.

"But, John . . ."

"Do as I say," Law said sharply.

"Best do as he says, Mrs. Gibbons," Dalrymple said with a smirk. "I'd hate to have to shoot a woman, even if she is a whore."

Law's jaw tightened and his blue-green eyes snapped fire, but those were the only outward signs of the anger that erupted inside of him.

"Come inside, Mrs. Gibbons," Judge Spellman said, taking the woman by the arm and tugging her toward the door. He had heard the commotion and had hurried out of his office to investigate.

"But, Henry . . ." Sara Jane protested. "I must help John Thomas. I don't know why they're . . ."

Spellman glared past Law's shoulder at Dalrymple. He wasn't sure whether the Pinkerton had any real reason to arrest Sara Jane's companion, but whatever the reason, he did not have to use such language in referring to Sara Jane.

"The best help you can give him right now is to get out of the way, Sara Jane," Spellman insisted.

"But . . ."

"We can do nothing for him right now, Sara Jane," Spellman snapped. "Now come inside where you'll be safe." He tugged the woman again, and when she started moving, he shoved her behind him.

"I don't know your name, mister," Spellman said quietly to Law's back, "but if you care for this woman, you'll submit. Depending on your circumstances—and if I know Dalrymple, they're probably suspect—I can maybe help you legally. But I can't do a damn thing if you're lying here dead."

Law acknowledged it with an almost imperceptible nod. It went against everything he was, everything he had become, everything he stood for to surrender to a man like Milt Dalrymple, an arrogant, pompous son of a bitch who could not be trusted for a moment. Especially when it was obvious that Dalrymple had a desire to avenge Law's treatment of him at Sara Jane's house the day Law and Tyler had arrived in St. Joseph.

Law's every instinct told him to fight this out—to die fighting, if he was going to die, rather than at the end of a rope—to make sure he got Dalrymple first. The man was a blight on humankind, and removing him would be a service to humanity.

But common sense began to reassert itself. He could not, he knew, even as good as he was, take out six men, five of whom had weapons out and cocked. Besides, he could not help Sara Jane if he were dead. He might not be of much help in jail, but there was always the chance that the judge could help him.

And, he decided, it was time to settle this once and for all in court. His indiscretions may have been serious, but they were few, really, and they had been a long time ago. And he had been law-abiding for many years now, indeed, was on the side of the law. With Spellman's help—and he believed the judge's promise—he might get this cleared up quickly. Then he would be done with Dalrymple and the Pinkertons, and he would be free to help Sara Jane, as well as forever be shed of the need to tread lightly outside of Texas.

"Pull your piece or surrender," Dalrymple snapped. He was enjoying being the center of attention of the crowd that had gathered. It was, he figured, as it should be.

Law gazed over the group arrayed before him. Besides Dalrymple, he recognized Dalrymple's partner, Ned Rogers, and William Iverson, the Pinkerton that Law had battered for tailing him. Iverson's face was still a mottled, swollen mess from the beating.

Then Law slowly raised his hands over his head, fighting back a small ripple of glee at seeing the disappointment spread rapidly across Dalrymple's face. But the feeling was fleeting because Law knew that Dalrymple's dissatisfaction would only turn to anger. That did not bode well for Law.

Dalrymple muttered, "Baxter," and when one of the Pinkertons looked at him, he jerked his head toward Law. Baxter edged up toward Law. He had heard of what Law had done with two hardened outlaws one time, and three another, and he was mighty nervous, just waiting for this big, broad-shouldered man to try something.

But Law simply let the Pinkerton take his two revolvers and big knife. He considered telling the man to relax, that he was not about to do anything, but decided to let the man sweat. He could see no reason to ease the man's discomfort.

Baxter tossed one of Law's pistols to another Pinkerton, and then the second. He stuffed the knife into his belt, then backed away, still aiming his own revolver at Law.

Dalrymple brought his right arm forward. What he had been holding over his shoulder were leg irons and handcuffs. He grinned maliciously at Law.

"Is that necessary?" Spellman asked. He had come outside again, standing just behind and to the right side of Law.

" 'Course it is, Judge," Dalrymple said with a smirk. "This here's a dangerous man. A mad-dog killer."

"Is that the charge?" Spellman queried.

"Well, no, can't say that's the exact charge, Judge," Dalrymple said, not liking this questioning of his authority, even by a judge.

"Then what is it?" Spellman demanded.

"The warrants were signed out for his part in a couple of bank robberies."

"Recent?"

"Well, no, not exactly."

Spellman continued glaring at the Pinkerton, then said, "You best make damn sure those warrants are in order, Mister Dalrymple."

"They are, Judge, they are," Dalrymple said, spitting to indicate his displeasure. He turned his head. "Would you like to do the honors, Mister Iverson?" he asked.

"Sure," the Pinkerton mumbled, his battered face making it difficult to talk. He uncocked his pistol and slid it into a coat pocket. He marched over to Dalrymple, took the two sets of irons, and moved much more slowly toward Law.

"I ain't fixin' to bite you, bub," Law said quietly.

Iverson glared at him, fear in his eyes, then snapped the handcuffs around Law's wrists. He knelt and locked the leg irons around Law's knee-high boots, at the ankles. Then Iverson rose and stepped back, pulling his gun from his pocket.

With the bounty man secured, Dalrymple strutted forward, stepped up on the boardwalk, and tried to go behind Law. But Spellman shifted and got in the way.

"Move, Judge," Dalrymple growled.

Spellman smiled insolently at the Pinkerton, then moved ever so slowly out of the way, into the doorway.

Dalrymple got behind Law, who was almost half a foot taller. "All right, asshole, move it," the Pinkerton said, shoving Law's back.

Law did not budge. Dalrymple pushed harder, but Law continued to resist, standing there as if rooted. When he felt Dalrymple pull back, Law waited a second, then stepped forward, off the boardwalk and a bit to the side, just as Dalrymple went to shove him again. The Pinkerton stumbled forward a half step and his cheek bumped into Law's back. Law kept going, clanking his way, and Dalrymple almost fell. He managed to right himself, flushing with anger as titters ricocheted around the crowd.

Seething, Dalrymple righted himself, then shoved Law again, even though the bounty man was moving forward, steadily, if slowly. The other Pinkertons fell in behind as they proceeded in a bizarre parade toward Marshal Al Fairburn's office.

Fairburn looked up sharply as a Pinkerton opened the door and stepped inside, followed by the shackled Law, then the procession of armed Pinkertons. Fairburn rose, anger coloring his face. Behind him, Deputy O'Connor also rose, hand resting on the grip of his pistol.

"What the hell's the meaning of this?" Fairburn demanded.

"This here's a wanted man, Marshal," Dalrymple said smugly. "A bank robber, consorter with the James gang, killer."

Fairburn looked toward Law, who stared, expressionless, back at him, giving nothing away. The marshal swung his head back to Dalrymple. "Those're mighty strong accusations, boy."

Dalrymple shrugged, his insolence rolling off him like fog off the Missouri River. "You weren't going to do your job, you useless scum, so I had to do it for you. Now open up one of your cells, so I can put this lawbreaking cuss away."

Out of the corner of his eye, Fairburn caught Law's almost imperceptible nod. It was obvious that the bounty man did not want the marshal or his deputy hurt on his account. "Unshackle him," Fairburn ordered, as he stroked one of the long, dangling ends of his straw-colored mustache.

"Not till he's locked up," Dalrymple insisted.

"Either unshackle him now, or you and your fellow rummies will be in the cell next to him," Fairburn said flatly. He was not about to be intimidated by Dalrymple or all the Pinkertons in the country.

"Don't push your luck, old man," Dalrymple snarled. "You're outgunned and outmanned."

Fairburn glared at him balefully, not too worried.

Law braced for trouble. Ned Rogers and one of the other Pinkertons were in striking range in the small office, and he could—and would—pound both if trouble broke out.

Then Dalrymple shrugged. He was furious, but he had enough sense to know that even if he survived a gunfight here in the marshal's office—one that would almost certainly kill the lawman and his deputy—it would end his career and almost any decent future he had imagined for himself. "All right, Mister Iverson," he said, "undo those irons."

Iverson nervously unlocked the arm and leg shackles and took them off. He laid the irons on the marshal's desk.

"All right, J.T.," Fairburn said, picking up a ring of keys from his desk, "let's go." He waved an arm toward the back of the room and the door that led to the four cells there.

Law stepped forward. Dalrymple and Rogers moved up to follow, but Fairburn blocked the Pinkertons' path. "Your presence ain't needed," he said firmly.

"That man is my prisoner," Dalrymple snapped, "and I aim to see that he's properly locked up."

Over his shoulder, Fairburn said to his deputy, "Earl, if any of these peckerwoods tries to follow me and J.T. into the back, shoot him."

"Yessir." O'Connor sounded almost eager.

"All right, J.T.," He turned and followed Law into the back.

"Which one?" Law asked. All four cells were empty, which surprised him a little. Then he remembered that Fairburn had released the ratty little man who had pointed Law out to his would-be killers in the Riverside, after putting the fear of God—and Law—into him.

"The one to your right has the best bed, such as it is, or so I'm told," Fairburn said.

Law walked into the first of four cells and turned as Fairburn closed and locked the door.

"I hate to do this, J.T.," Fairburn said with sincere apology in his voice.

"I know, Al."

"I'll look into this and see what I can find out. Maybe I might could be able to help you."

"Obliged. I'd be even more so if you'd keep watch over Sara Jane."

Fairburn nodded. He turned to head out, then turned back. "Is anything of what that asshole said true?" he asked.

"Some," Law admitted. He sighed. He didn't like to talk about it, but he thought Fairburn deserved some explanation. "After the war, things was bad in Texas, as you well know," he said evenly. "After S . . . my fiancee cast me over because of . . . well, that ain't important. It's just that at the time, I had nothin'. My folks died of fever, and their place was sold by the goddamn Yankees for taxes. I didn't know what to do with myself. As a former Reb—and one who'd rode with Quantrill and Bloody Bill—I couldn't expect to have much of a future with the Blue Bellies running everything. So I made the damnfool decision to come on back up this way. I'd heard Jesse and Frank had joined with Cole Younger and his brothers and they were all still fightin' the war, in a manner of speaking. Or, at least they were robbin' rich Yankees. So I joined up with 'em."

Fairburn shook his head. He could understand in some way why Law had done it, but it was, as Law himself admitted, a damnfool thing. And it might just make getting Law out of this predicament a sight harder. Fairburn tugged at his mustache. "How long did you ride with those boys?" he asked.

"Few months is all. Just went on a couple of ventures with 'em. I was powerful ashamed of what they—we— were doing. I did some mighty awful things during the War of Northern Aggression, but they seemed right at the time. Ridin' with Jesse and Cole didn't. So I took my leave of 'em and went on back to Texas."

"And became a bounty man, eh?" Fairburn almost smiled.

"After a spell." Law hesitated, then added, "There was some lost years in there, Marshal."

"None of this seems so bad to me, J.T.," Fairburn said after a few seconds of thought. "I reckon we can work something out in court. It ain't as if you were still robbin' banks last week." He cocked an eyebrow in question at the prisoner. "Unless you been lyin' about this."

"Nope."

"Then, I expect we can do something. I'll look into it."

"Thanks, Marshal."

Law took off his heavy coat, tossed it into a corner, and sat on the hard bunk. He could hear Fairburn and the Pinkertons jabbering away, but before long, the front door of the office opened, then slammed shut, and it was quiet.

An hour later, Fairburn poked his head through the door and said, "Mrs. Gibbons is here to see you."

"No," Law said flatly. "It's bad enough she had to see me arrested like that. I sure as hell don't want her to see me in here."

"She don't deserve such treatment from you."

"That's right, I don't," Sara Jane said, pushing past Fairburn into the cell block. She marched up to the cell door. "Open this door, Marshal," she commanded. "I want to talk to Mister Law without bars between us."

"I can't do that, Mrs. Gibbons," Fairburn said without too much conviction. "You know that."

"Do you think he'll try to escape, Marshal?"

"Well, no, not really, I expect." He glanced at Law. "You're not gonna try to escape, are you?"

"Nope."

"Well, then," Sara Jane insisted.

"All right, all right, ma'am."

CHAPTER 16

LAW ROSE AS Sara Jane entered the cell. She smiled at him and perched on the edge of the bunk. She patted the area next to her. "Sit, John Thomas," she said quietly.

"You certain?" he asked dubiously.

Sara Jane nodded. When he sat, leaving a little space between them, she asked, "What's this all about, John Thomas?"

"You don't want to know that, Sara Jane," he said, voice almost pained. If there was anyone in the world he did not want to confess these past sins to, it was this woman.

"Yes, I do, John Thomas," she said firmly, looking at him with eyes that made him want to . . . He wasn't sure what. He could not possibly love her any more than he already did.

Law quickly explained it, just as he had to Fairburn only an hour ago.

When Law had finished, Sara Jane said, "I'll speak to Judge Spellman. I'm sure he'll be able to help."

"I don't want you getting involved in all this, Sara Jane," Law said. "It's too dangerous—to your reputation, even if not physically. Marshal Fairburn said he'd do what he could. That should be good enough."

"Now you listen to me, John Thomas Law," Sara Jane said with iron in her voice, "I am involved. Have been since . . . well, since you and Mister Tyler rode into town. If it wasn't for me, you wouldn't even have come to St. Joe, and you wouldn't be sitting in this jail right now, waiting to pay for sins that happened half a lifetime ago."

"Now don't go getting . . ."

"I'm not finished, sir," Sara Jane said harshly. "You have done so much for me in the short time you've been here. You've protected me, protected my reputation, protected my children. You have done nothing that has not been in my best interest—or the best interests of my children. Now it is you who are in need of some help, and I will give it, if there is any way I can. I owe you that much. And more."

"But, Sara Jane . . ."

"Hush, John Thomas," she said more quietly, pressing a finger to his lips. She was surprised at the jolt of heat it sent through her. "I love my husband dearly, John Thomas. He's a good man. He really is."

To Law it almost sounded as if she were trying to convince herself more than him.

"But just because you and me parted ways so long ago doesn't mean all my feelings for you died. They're still there, even after all these years."

His heart jumped . . .

"They're maybe not nearly as strong as they were then, but they're still there."

. . . And fell . . .

"If it wasn't for my feelings for Oliver, I would . . ."

"Enough of such talk, Sara Jane," Law finally said. He could not take this rising and plunging of his hope. It was too hard on him, and he was sure it was just as tough on her.

She looked at him with tear-filled eyes.

"Go on home, Sara Jane," Law said, trying to keep the pain out of his voice. "Let's see if Marshal Fairburn can help me. If he doesn't seem to be able to, then maybe you can talk to Judge Spellman. For the time being, though, you best go on home and watch over the young'uns. And continue with your plans to leave for Texas."

"I'm not sure that's a good idea anymore, John Thomas," Sara Jane said, dabbing at her eyes with a linen hankie.

"It is a good idea," Law insisted. "Maybe now even more than before. If the marshal and Judge Spellman can help me, I should be out of here soon, and we can head on to Texas. If, for some reason, they can't, then I won't be around to protect you no more, and getting you to Texas will be even more important."

She shuddered at the thought of him dying. It would be too much for her to bear. But she could see the logic in his suggestion. She nodded. "All right, John Thomas," she said, rising. "But that marshal best do something right quick." She reached up and patted his cheek.

Once again desire for this woman swept over him like a prairie fire. He gritted his teeth to keep from doing something rash. Then she spun and walked out of the cell and was gone. He breathed again.

A moment later, Fairburn walked back in and locked the door. Neither man could think of anything to say, so neither said anything.

A few hours later, however, the marshal returned, this time carrying a sizeable basket. Behind him was Deputy O'Connor. Fairburn unlocked the cell door and carried the basket inside. "Supper," he announced with a grin.

O'Connor put a large coffeepot down on the floor next to the bed, and two tin mugs.

Law, who had been lying down, sat up, took the basket, and peeled away the cloth that covered it. Inside was a small covered pot from which a delightful aroma wafted. Law took the metal cover off to find a savory stew full of meat and thick gravy. There were also half a dozen biscuits, a small crockery cup of butter, a large slice of peach pie, a dull knife, and a spoon and fork. He looked up at Fairburn. "Looks mighty fine," he said, taste buds working overtime in anticipation.

"That's good grub there, boy," Fairburn said with another grin. "Comes from Cooperman's, the finest eatin' establishment in St. Joseph."

"How do I rate such fare?" Law asked.

"The Pinkertons don't know it yet, but they're payin' for it," Fairburn said with a laugh. "If Dalrymple's gonna be such an ass, he's gonna pay for it one way or t'other." He nodded thanks as O'Connor brought in a chair, which Fairburn set in the middle of the cell and plopped into.

Law grinned. "Want some?" he asked.

"Already et. Same as you got. I figured if we was gettin' grub from such a fine place, me and Earl ought to be included. I will take me some coffee, though."

Seeing as how he was as hungry as a spring bear, Law dug into the meal with gusto. Afterward, he broke out two slim cigars and gave one to Fairburn. They fired them up and relaxed, puffing away, slurping coffee. They talked little, and when they did, it was of not much importance.

Before he left, though, Fairburn said, "This was some enjoyable, J.T., but I reckon it won't happen again. It wouldn't look right if we was to be seen, and I expect those damned Pinkertons to be nosin' 'round some the next couple of days, at least."

Law nodded, understanding. "Your company was welcome, Al, but there's no need to cause yourself grief. You do what you got to do." He grinned. "But I could use some more cigars."

"I'll see to it." Fairburn turned and sadly left the cell. He had come to like John Thomas Law and was ashamed to be even a small part of Law's present troubles.

MORNING BROUGHT ANOTHER fine meal—fresh hen's eggs, a slab of ham, a goodly portion of biscuits and gravy. And more coffee, of course. Plus Fairburn had brought him a handful of the slim cigars he favored. With the exception that he was locked up, which was, of course, a mighty big exception, the day was off to a fine start.

His buoyant mood soured in a hurry, however, when Milt Dalrymple and Ned Rogers showed up a couple of hours later. The two did not look happy as they plunked chairs down just outside Law's cell.

Fairburn poked his head through the doorway, nodded solemnly at Law, then closed the door.

Law wondered if the marshal was listening through the closed door. He pulled out a cigar and lit it.

"Did you have a good evening in your new digs?" Dalrymple asked. He was clean-shaven and well-dressed, as usual, with a sharp white shirt, silk vest, string tie, and town frock coat.

"I've had worse nights," Law allowed. He blew a stream of smoke at the two Pinkertons.

"And you'll have lots more," Dalrymple said. He paused, then grinned maliciously. "Well, I reckon that's not true," he added. "Not when I aim to make sure you're the main guest at a necktie party."

"That so?" Law countered nonchalantly.

"That's so, asshole," Dalrymple said nastily. He sneered.

"If those charges from your days with Jesse James and his rabble ain't enough to make sure you get your neck stretched, there's always the threats you made against me and Ned here. Plus attacking a Pinkerton, like you did with poor Iverson, won't help you none."

Law shrugged. "I expect you're going to find that ain't too many people 'round here have much liking for you and your clap-ridden partners," he said evenly.

Dalrymple seemed unfazed. He did not believe Law. "You'll be the one surprised, boy," he said almost cheerfully. "Most folks—most God-fearin', law-abidin' folks anyways—like good lawmen, not chicken-hearted cusses like Fairburn."

"You could live to be as old as Methuselah and you still wouldn't be half the lawman that Al Fairburn is," Law declared.

"He's an offense to real crime-fighters like me," Dalrymple said arrogantly.

Law shook his head. He could see no point in arguing. Dalrymple was too arrogant, too self-important to see that he would never be a truly good lawman, in large part because his delusions of greatness were so powerful.

"You might be able to convince that rummy of a marshal that that gunplay you engaged in outside Bzovys' store and in the Riverside were self-defense, but you ain't going to convince a jury of it," Dalrymple said. "It'll just show you for the bloodthirsty bastard you are."

"It's not likely you'll find a jury in these parts that'd be willin' to hang a man for killin' some scum like those I sent to the boneyard."

Dalrymple smiled evilly. "I reckon you're thinkin' that since you talked that dumb son of a bitch judge into bein' on your side, that you're gonna just stroll out of a courtroom a free man. But I'll tell you this, pard—It ain't gonna happen."

"Oh?" Law wasn't sure Spellman could help him, but it would be a good thing to have a judge on his side, even to some extent, in a courtroom.

"I aim to see that Judge Spellman, that idiot, won't be presiding at your trial, Law. Should be easy enough to talk another court into taking jurisdiction because of that bastard's connection to you."

For the first time, Law began to worry. He figured Dalrymple could manage that if he put his mind to it. Still, the Pinkertons would have a tough row to hoe, even with the charges of robbery. They were old charges, and he thought a jury would be forgiving, since he had lived on the side of the law since. Plus, with a marshal and a judge to vouch for him, he was still pretty certain that he would be exonerated.

"But get this through your thick head, Law: I will see you hang. If we think a jury might have doubts about any of the charges we bring—or if we get a judge who's as soft-headed as Spellman—I am planning to level other, more serious charges against you."

"There are none," Law said flatly. He did not like where this was headed.

"There will be," Dalrymple said, with a ruthless smile. "As many as I think it'll take to send you to the gallows."

Law believed him.

Dalrymple's evil grin grew. "And while you're waiting on your trial, I'll be whiling away my time with that fine filly you been sharing quarters with," he said with a leer.

Law fought with all his might to keep his face expressionless and battle the flames of fury that had burst forth inside of him.

"Now, I admit, she ain't so young anymore," Dalrymple went on, his lips twisting further into a thick, lascivious smile that gave him the look of a serpent. "But goddamn, I bet that whore is a juicy thing. I can't wait till I get my hands on her naked ass. Lord almighty, I'd wager her tits're fine—all plump and large with womanliness." Oiliness poured off him like water over a falls. "I'm almost jealous of you, pard," he added, "livin' with her in that big old house like you been, her husband gone missing. Yessir, must be near heaven. But I'll find out soon enough."

It took what seemed like a week for Law to control his rage and be able to speak. "Marshal!" he shouted. When Fairburn popped through the door a second later, Law said, "Mister Asswipe here says he'd like to come into my cell, by himself, to talk. I'm willin'."

Dalrymple blanched. His arrogance might cause him to do stupid things at times, but this was not one of them. Law had the size and strength—and the rage—to mash him to a bloody pulp if he went into that cell. "That's not true, Marshal," he said, standing so fast that he knocked his chair over. "Agent Rogers and I were just leaving." With his partner in tow, Dalrymple hurried out of the room.

"Please fetch Sara Jane for me, Marshal," Law said tightly.

Fairburn nodded and left. Twenty anxious minutes later, Sara Jane showed up, looking pale and frightened. Fairburn let her into the cell and then returned to the office out front.

"What's wrong, John Thomas?" Sara Jane asked.

While he had waited for her, Law had considered how much to tell her, and he had decided to say nothing about Dalrymple's designs on her. At least not yet. "The Pinkertons really have it in for me, Sara Jane," he said evenly, "to the point where I figure they're fixing to trump up some charges against me to make sure I hang."

"But Judge Spellman will . . ."

"They're fixing to make sure he's not the judge at my trial, too," he said hastily. "And I think they can do it."

"So what do we do?"

"I need to get out of here, Sara Jane, and *pronto*. I don't figure the Pinkertons're going to wait long before they bring me into court. A few days, a week, maybe, at most. What I need you to do is send a wire to a Mister D.J. Howard in Nashville, Tennessee. Tell him I'm in jail here and need to get out soon. Ask if he can get some of his friends here to help."

"Who is this fellow?" Sara Jane asked, her worry deepening.

"Never you mind, girl," Law said more harshly than he had intended. But he needed Sara Jane to act, not stand around asking questions.

She stared at him a few moments, fear, worry, concern—and, yes, love—flickering across her face. Then she nodded. She touched his cheek as she had the last time, spun, and hurried out.

As Law sat there considering just walking out of the still-open cell door and trying to talk or bribe his way past Fairburn, the marshal came in and locked the cell. He said nothing as he went back into the outer office.

Early in the evening, Sara Jane returned. Fairburn did not come with her to open the cell, but Law didn't give it much thought at the moment. He simply asked, "Well?"

"Arrangements are being made," Sara Jane said, almost breathlessly. "There's much to be done yet, but be ready day after tomorrow, right around this time."

Law pulled out his watch and clicked it open, eliciting a sharp intake of breath from Sara Jane, as she recognized it as the one she had given him when she was seventeen and they were planning marriage. Law offered her a small smile. "I'd as soon die as give this up, Sara Jane," he said very softly.

Her face flushed with pride . . . or was it love? She wasn't sure. She smiled back at him, then said, "I must go, John Thomas." Holding her index and middle fingers together, she kissed them, then pressed them to his mouth. A moment later she was gone.

The touch lingered on his lips for a long time, and he fell asleep with thoughts of her flooding his mind.

He spent the next two days pacing his cell, wanting out immediately, but knowing that could not happen, though knowing, too, that he would be free soon. He considered trying to warn Fairburn, obliquely, that something was imminent—after all, he did not want the marshal getting hurt when he was broken out of jail. But to warn him, even obliquely, would only make matters worse, he thought.

LAW ALMOST WORE out the watch as he kept checking the time on the day it was supposed to happen. It seemed that time moved with all the rapidity of a snail swimming in a pool of molasses in February. But finally the door between the offices and the cell area opened and he heard the words he had been waiting for: "Time to go, John Thomas."

CHAPTER 17

"Sara Jane?" Law sputtered. He was incredulous.

He almost didn't recognize her as she was clad in a long, heavy wool coat under which it seemed she was wearing men's trousers. Her hair was tucked up under a Stetson with a tall crown. She pulled off thick gloves as she walked to the cell.

"Yes, John Thomas," she said quietly. She hurriedly unlocked the door and shoved it open. "Come, we don't have much time."

"But how . . . ? Why . . . ? What . . . ?" He had never been so shocked, so utterly flabbergasted. He could not believe his eyes, and he began to suspect he was having some kind of bizarre dream.

"There's no time for that now, John Thomas," Sara Jane said urgently. "We must go. Now. I'll explain everything later."

"No," he said, fighting to regain his senses.

"What do you mean, no?" she demanded. "John Thomas, this is no time to be hardheaded."

"I can't let you do this, Sara Jane," he said. "It's . . ."

"It's what?" she countered. "Necessary? The right thing to do?"

"Dangerous," he snapped. "And fool-headed."

"Fiddle-faddle," she said in agitation. "Do you remember what I said to you the other day—just after they put you in here?"

"I reckon." He wasn't sure what she was getting at.

"Well, I meant it. I care for you, John Thomas. Maybe not in the same way I once did, but there's been so long a separation between us, that that's to be expected. But you mean very much to me. Very much. And I owe you so very much for all you've done for me in the short time you've been in St. Joe."

"But you live here, and . . ."

"You were planning to take me back to Texas, remember?" Sara Jane countered. "That's not going to change. We just change the way—and the time—we're going to do that. And, you were right, things are getting worse. Since you were put in this jail, the Pinkertons have become growing pests. That one, Dalrymple," she added with a shudder of fear and disgust, "has been coming 'round every few hours during the day, and I think he might've tried to get into the house last night. It's . . ."

Law made up his mind the instant Sara Jane had mentioned Dalrymple and what the Pinkerton was trying to do. The words chilled his heart. He knew that the Pinkerton would keep his word about moving in on Sara Jane as soon as he thought he could get away with it. Law just hadn't expected the man to try it so obviously and so soon.

"You're right, Sara Jane," Law interrupted. "It's time to go." He grabbed his coat, pushed past her into the hallway, and then went through the doorway into the office. He stopped and looked around. There were no bodies, no blood. He looked quizzically at Sara Jane as she moved up next to him.

"I'll explain it all later," she said again. "Now go get your pistols. I hope we don't need them, but . . ." she tapered off.

Law knelt in front of the safe, which was unlocked, the door ajar. Things were getting more curious by the minute, he thought as he reached in and pulled out the two Colts, with holsters, and four boxes of shells that were sitting right there. He strapped the holsters on after making sure the revolvers were loaded, then put on his caped greatcoat. Both pairs of gloves were in the pockets. He pulled on the pair from which he had cut out the fingertips, then picked up the boxes of cartridges from where he had set them on the desk and stuck them in his coat pockets. He turned and looked at Sara Jane. She was pale with fright, but her face showed determination. "Ready?" he asked.

She nodded and headed for the door. Law clapped his hat on and was right behind her as she went out into the frigid night. She turned left and he followed, down to the end of the building, around the corner, down the slight space between the marshal's office and the millinery next door, and into the alley at back. She turned right, stumbling a little in the darkness, broken only by the pale full moon. She turned again and again, Law blindly following her, holding onto the cape of her coat. Finally she stopped. Law had no idea where they were. He wasn't sure if they were on a street or another alley, but there was an oil lamp throwing some light.

A woman—at least Law thought it was a woman; he couldn't be sure in the low light and with the way she was dressed—waited with Sara Jane's three children, all of them bundled up against the freezing air; four horses, including Toby; and two mules. The horses were saddled, and the mules were laden with supplies.

"I was getting a little nervous," the waiting woman said. She was holding little Walter in her arms. The boy seemed to be asleep.

"I know, Judith," Sara Jane said. "I think it was something of a surprise to John Thomas to see me."

"That's putting it mildly," Law said dryly. Once he had made up his mind to go along with Sara Jane, his reason had returned, and he was thinking of the possibilities and what would have to be done. It had surprised him a little to see the children here, though after a moment's thought, he realized it should not have. Sara Jane could not be expected to leave them behind. Even if she could leave them with this woman, whom she must have trusted implicitly, that would put this woman and her husband in jeopardy. No, as soon as he thought it through, it was obvious that he and Sara Jane would have to travel with the children. At least for a while. He would figure out how to get them to Texas as quickly and as safely as possible sometime later.

However, it dawned on him that traveling with one child not far removed from infancy and one who was still quite young might not be that easy for people on the run.

"You sure you want to go through with this, Sara Jane?" he asked. "It ain't too late for you to go on back home and let me escape on my own." His stomach twisted even as he said it—if she went home, and he was on the run, Sara Jane would have no protection from Milt Dalrymple.

"Of course. Being on the run won't be easy. I know that, John Thomas," she said. "But it'll be a sight better than being left to whatever evils Mister Dalrymple has in store for me." She smiled. "Besides, I'll be with you."

Warmth splashed over him. "But the children," he said. "It'll be powerful hard on them."

"I know," Sara Jane said as she helped Janie onto a small pinto. "As you well know, I can ride like the true Texan I am, and I've taught Lem and Janie to be comfortable on horseback. Walter'll ride with me. Janie might get a bit tired, but we'll have to deal with it as best we can."

Law nodded. It was the best they could do for now. His

real concern was the weather. The children might be able to ride fine, but it was bitter cold these nights, and he worried how they would fare.

"We'll be fine, Mister Law," Lemuel said as he mounted his horse, a chestnut. He sounded determined. "Won't we, Janie?"

The nine-year-old gave a firm nod.

Despite the seriousness of the situation, Law had to smile. He felt a bit of pride in Sara Jane for the fine job she had done in raising her children. "All right, then," he said, moving up to Toby and giving the horse a lump of sugar. He was rewarded with a soft snicker.

Law pulled himself into the saddle and watched as the woman—whom he now recognized as Judge Spellman's wife—handed Walter up to Sara Jane. "Which way's north?" he asked.

Sara Jane, holding Walter on the saddle in front of her, pointed. "Why?" she asked, a bit surprised.

"That's the way we're heading," Law said, having just made the decision.

"Texas is the other way," Sara Jane said, confused.

"You know that, and I know that," Law said slowly. "And the Pinkertons know that. First place they're going to look for us is south, figuring that we'll have hightailed it for Kansas City and the train. They'll wire every train depot from here to Austin to be on the watch for us."

"Oh," Sara Jane said sheepishly.

"Don't fret on it, Sara Jane," Law said soothingly. "I'm used to thinking of such things, with the way I make my living."

"So you really are a bounty man?" she asked. There was no derision in her voice.

Law nodded. "I've been doing it a long spell now, and I've gotten damn . . . er, darn . . . good at it."

"Won't the Pinkertons think the same and wire ahead to places north of here?"

"Might," Law allowed. "But it's still safer, I reckon. From what I can recall, there aren't many places of any size north of here for some distance. But I also think they'll figure, once they've determined that you've helped me, that somehow we'd be trying to get you to Kansas City as quick as possible and on the train to Texas. They might not know where I am, and might figure I've gone north, but I'd wager that they'd go looking for you, thinking that once they've got you—and the young'uns—in custody that either I'll come back for you when word gets out, or that they'll force you to tell them where I've gone off to. I doubt they'll figure that we'd be traveling together."

Sara Jane hoped he was right.

"Lem," Law said, "your ma has her hands full with Walter, and I need to be ready to protect us should something happen. Would you mind taking the lines to the pack mules?"

"No, sir, I wouldn't mind a'tall," Lemuel said, proud that Law had seen fit to entrust him with such an important task.

"Thank you for all your help, Judith," Sara Jane said to her friend.

The woman nodded. "You mind that you keep out of trouble," Judith said.

Law tipped his hat to the woman. "Lead on, Sara Jane."

Sara Jane pulled out, followed by Janie, then Lemuel leading the two mules. Law waited a few seconds to let them get a little ahead, then moved on himself, bringing up the rear where he could keep watch, though it seemed unnecessary at the moment.

Once they were out of the city, Law urged Sara Jane to pick up the pace a little. They needed to put some distance between them and any possible pursuit, though Law figured there would be none until after dawn, if at all. He still figured that any pursuit would head south.

By midnight, Walter was asleep in Sara Jane's arms, and Sara Jane herself and her daughter Janie were fighting to keep awake. Law was too keyed up and alert to be tired, and it seemed like Lemuel was doing well, too. Law did not want to stop, but he knew they had to, for the sake of the horses, if not the children. He quickly rode up past Sara Jane and scouted ahead a little ways. The sound of the Missouri had faded as the road moved away from the river, which Law found a blessing.

Finally he found a copse of trees along a frozen-over creek. He went back and led the others to the spot. Sara Jane found a dry spot and lay Walter down on a couple of blankets, Janie curled up next to him, and their mother covered them with more blankets. Law and Lemuel unloaded the mules, then Law unsaddled the horses and began tending them, while Lemuel and his mother gathered firewood and built a fire. Sara Jane put coffee on, while Lemuel went to help Law, who nodded his appreciation. The boy grinned.

After one cup of hot coffee, Lemuel burrowed into the blankets with his brother and sister. Law and Sara Jane sat at the fire, appreciating its heat and sipping more coffee.

"So, tell me how you came to be my rescuer, Sara Jane," Law finally said.

"After I talked with you the other night, when you told me to contact Jesse James . . ."

"You knew that D.J. Howard is Jesse James?" Law asked, surprised again. "I had only heard it a couple of days ago, overhearing some fellah in a saloon."

"I didn't know it when you told me to wire him. When I left you, Marshal Fairburn stopped me. He had heard what we were talking about."

"That fellah can't be trusted," Law groused.

"Hush. Anyway, he told me who Mister Howard was, which put me in quite the fix, John Thomas," she scolded. "I couldn't in good conscience seek help from a man like Jesse James, but I couldn't let you stay in jail."

"So you concocted this scheme?"

"Well, yes," Sara Jane said with a small laugh. "But not right away. First, Marshal Fairburn told me that he had heard your talk with Mister Dalrymple that morning. He told me what Dalrymple is—was—planning, both about you, and about me."

Law's eyes narrowed in anger, but he said nothing.

"The marshal was furious. He wanted to do something about it, but there wasn't anything he could do legally, that we could see. And he certainly couldn't just shoot Dalrymple, though I would have thanked him if he had." She smiled wanly. She was tired and wanted to sleep, but Law deserved an explanation.

"Sometimes working separate from the law is better," Law commented.

"You might be right," Sara Jane muttered. "That's when I came up with the idea. Or at least the beginnings of it. Plans were already being made for me—us—to go back to Texas, of course. I figured it would just have to happen sooner. I hinted to the marshal that I might want to try to help you escape somehow. He didn't mind helping you, but he wasn't keen on the idea of me helping. Too dangerous, he told me. Still, he wanted to do something. He couldn't see you being punished for things you had done so long ago. Even more, he was revolted by what the Pinkertons—or at least Dalrymple and a couple of others—were planning. He eventually realized that either he had to do something directly, which would have caused no end of trouble, or he had to let me take part, and help as much as he could. So we came up with the idea together, really."

"Is that why he wasn't there and the safe with my pistols was open?"

Sara Jane nodded. She inched closer to the fire. "He told me he and his deputies would be busy at that time for no more than half an hour. It was difficult making all the arrangements in so short a time, but it had to be done. Judge Spellman wanted to help, too, but couldn't get involved directly, either. But he agreed to take over all the details of settling my affairs and dealing with the house, which made it a mite easier."

She sighed, glad now that the difficult part was over. "We had thought of waiting a couple more days, but Marshal Fairburn started getting suspicious that the Pinkertons were going to do something soon."

"I don't know what to say, Sara Jane," Law said. "I am in your debt for all time."

"No, John Thomas," she said, gazing at him. "What I did was only a small return on all you've done for me."

Law sat there silently for a while, then said, "You do know, don't you, Sara Jane, that things are going to be mighty tough for a long spell?"

"I hadn't really thought about it, John Thomas," Sara Jane said tiredly. "But I expect you're right." She smiled again, softly, warmly, life lighting up her face. "I'll say, though, that none of that matters now."

CHAPTER 18

LAW HATED TO do it, but he pushed them as hard as he could. It was difficult for the children, especially, which made it all the tougher on Sara Jane. After two full days, the two younger children began complaining frequently, which wore on Law's nerves, even though he continued to lag the group by a little distance, keeping watch. Lemuel handled things pretty well, but by the fourth day, even the determined lad was showing signs of strain.

That night, after the children had fallen asleep, Law and Sara Jane sat around the fire, as had become their custom. "Can we take a break here, John Thomas?" Sara Jane asked. "Maybe stay a day or two?" She was tired and unaccustomed to such travel. She was not used to cooking much at all, let alone over an open fire, or sitting in a saddle day after day. She had always had help with the children and the household chores, and plenty of comforts.

"That wouldn't be wise, Sara Jane," Law said. He knew how hard it had been on them, and he also knew it was going to only get more difficult. They were in territory he did not know and it was the middle of the winter. "We're still too close to St. Joe."

Sara Jane nodded, pulling the blanket a little tighter around her shoulders. She wanted to cry but was too tired.

Law reached out and stroked her cheek. "I know it's mighty hard on you—and the young'uns, Sara Jane," he said. "But to stop would be too dangerous."

"I suppose you're right," Sara Jane said with a weary sigh. She had never been so tired, so overwhelmed.

He was beginning to regret having embarked on this journey, at least with Sara Jane and the children. The more he thought about it, the angrier he got—at himself. He had endangered this woman and her children, just so that he could get away. If only he had had more time to have thought this through. If only she had let him know what she was planning so that he could have thought out the consequences. If only . . .

He fought back his anger. There were always "if onlys." He could not blame Sara Jane, nor could he even, really, fault his own thinking on this. A decision had had to be made immediately. He had made the right choice for the moment, he supposed. But it still did not sit well with him. Trouble was, there was nothing he could do to change it now. He could not send Sara Jane and the children back, nor could he send them on their way by themselves while he returned to St. Joseph and surrendered. No, they would have to push on.

"I'm sorry, Sara Jane," he said softly.

"For what?" She looked at him a little surprised.

"For bringing you out here into this wilderness, putting you and the children in such dire circumstances."

"It couldn't be helped, John Thomas," she responded, smiling weakly at him. "Not with what happened and how quickly."

"I know that, but . . ."

"What could we have done differently?"

"I reckon I could've left you and the young'uns in the care of Judge Spellman or Marshal Fairburn, then ridden like hell for Texas all on my own. You'd have been safe, and I would've been a heap farther away by now."

"Safe? Fiddle-faddle, John Thomas," Sara Jane said sharply. "If either of those men had thought he could protect us from Milt Dalrymple and his mad Pinkertons, we wouldn't have had to help you escape. Judge Spellman might've been able to help keep you from . . . from being hanged, but we couldn't take that chance. And besides, while we haven't seen hide nor hair of Ellsworth and his gang, they're still a danger to me and the children." She paused. "And even Oliver," she added in what sounded even to her like a far-off voice.

"I reckon," Law said dubiously.

"We did what we had to do, John Thomas," Sara Jane said quietly, though with a note of conviction. "There's no going back now, so we'll just go on and do the best we can." She smiled with a fierce determination. "We're Texans, John Thomas. Through and through. And we have no give-up in us."

Law's lips curled into a respectful grin. "You are one hell of a woman, Sara Jane," he said. He knew how difficult all this was for her—how easy a life she had led, both with a rich father and later with a well-off judge for a husband. His love could grow no stronger for her, but his desire for her could, and did.

She flushed with pleasure.

AT MIDMORNING THE next day, Law spotted a crudely lettered sign announcing that there was a ferry across the

Missouri River four miles west. He galloped ahead to Sara Jane and stopped her. He tugged the scarf down off of his lower face and asked, "Did you see the sign?"

She nodded, her face looking weather-battered. It was a raw, blustery, frigid day, and it was telling on all of them.

"I think we should take it."

Sara Jane nodded again.

"How're you doing, little guy?" Law asked, reaching out and poking Walter, who was bundled up from toes to head. All that could really be seen were two watery brown eyes peeking out of wrappings.

"All right," the boy said, his voice so muffled by a scarf that it was almost unintelligible.

Law turned them west and got them moving. He swiftly rode back and threw a rope around the sign, yanked it down, and dragged it along the barely discernible trail a little, then back behind some rocks. He dismounted, retrieved his rope, and then trotted until he caught up with the others.

Within an hour they came to a battered shack. A thin plume of smoke rose from a rickety stone chimney. On the far side of the cabin was a small barn that was tilted considerably to one side. On the near side, close to the edge of the icy river, a flat-bottomed ferry sat up on several logs.

"Hello!" Law shouted after pulling the scarf away from his mouth. "Hello the house!

Moments later, the shack's door opened and a short, rotund man wearing a tattered wool coat, threadbare wool pants, and moth-eaten slouch hat stepped out. The huge walrus mustache parted as he warily asked, "What can I do fer y'all?"

"We need to get across the river," Law said. "When I saw your sign a ways back, I was hoping you could ferry us over." He chucked his chin toward the boat. "But that doesn't bode well for it."

"River's froze over clear 'cross," the man said. "Y'all can just amble on over to t'other side."

"It safe?" Law asked dubiously.

"I've done it more'n a few times. There's been winters when it ain't froze over quite so solid, but this year it's purt' solid."

Law considered that for a few moments. He glanced around, taking in the bundled-up faces of Sara Jane and the children. They would have to risk it, he supposed. There was nowhere else that would be any better, he figured.

"How's about you lead us over there, mister?" Law asked.

"Reckon I ain't so inclined to make that much effort," the man said with a shrug.

"How much you charge for ferrying folks in good weather?" Law asked.

"Twenty-five cent each person," he said, then added with a glare, "includin' young'uns." He continued in a more normal tone: "Fifty cent a horse or mule, a dollar fer a small wagon, two dollar fer a bigger wagon." He wondered why this big, hard-eyed stranger wanted to know.

"That'd be four dollars and twenty-five cents," Law allowed.

The man figured in his head for a bit, then nodded.

"I'll give you twenty bucks to lead us across."

The man's eyes widened. While he did all right ferrying people, animals, and wagons across the river during the summer months, his was still a remote outpost for such a business, and twenty dollars, especially here in the dead of winter, was a considerable sum. "Y'all wait there just one minute," he said, as he turned and hurried toward the barn.

He returned quickly, towing a massive draft horse by a rope around the animal's neck. He stopped next to Law. "If'n Millie here can make it across, that ice'll sure be strong enough for any of you and your animals," he said. He held out a gloved hand.

Law almost smiled as he handed the man a twenty-dollar gold piece that he had pulled from a coat pocket while the ferry man was in the barn. He had figured such a man would prefer hard money rather than greenbacks.

The man took the coin, eyed it suspiciously, then nodded in satisfaction. He dropped it into a pocket, then walked the big horse to a two-foot-tall tree stump. He climbed onto it and launched himself onto the horse's back. "Best spread out some," he said, looking back over the group, "lest we put too much weight on any one spot." He turned to face forward and clopped slowly off.

Law looked at Sara Jane, whose eyes were big with concern. "It'll be all right, Sara Jane," he said. Lemuel looked a bit worried, but not too bad. Janie appeared to be too tired and cold to care much, and Walter was too young to know the potential danger. Law gently kicked Toby's sides with his heels and moved off. The others followed, spreading out a little.

The crossing was uneventful, though their imaginations at times gave them a little cause for worry. But then they were on solid ground on the other side.

The ferry man had pulled to the side and sat on the big draft horse. "Y'all're in Nebraska now," he said as Law stopped next to him and the others filed past. "The Big Nemaha River's just a bit north of here. Y'all might want to foller it to keep your bearin's."

Law nodded. "Obliged," he said. He joined the others. He took the ferryman's advice and found the Big Nemaha River and followed its course west and a little north for more than two days.

The weather eased a bit, making the travel minimally easier. Law did not know what was out here; he just hoped he would be able to find someplace where they might rest for a while with little fear of discovery. The children were beginning to suffer, and Sara Jane looked exhausted. He was growing testy, angry at himself. Despite Sara Jane's words, and the knowledge that she was right, he still blamed himself for having gotten them into this. And he was getting nervous about the children's well-being. He didn't think he could live with himself if something happened to any of them out here.

But there was nothing but snow- and ice-covered prairie rolling out ahead of them. On the third day, he turned them south, making the move on nothing more than instinct.

They plodded on, wrapped heavily against the steady wind that often rose to a howl around them. The temperature rarely if ever got above freezing. Snow spit at them from time to time. Though they usually had enough wood, making meals was still an onerous chore, with Sara Jane being so tired, cold, and worn down and having to take care of her children. Eating was little better, as the food grew cold almost as soon as it was taken from the fire.

Law was in fine condition physically, but he had more than enough to do with saddling, unsaddling, and tending to all the horses and mules, loading and unloading their steadily shrinking store of supplies. Lemuel helped when he could, but the weather and constant travel had sapped his strength and energy.

Four days after turning south, on an afternoon that had been steadily turning from bright and sunny to gray and ominous, they spotted a number of tendrils of smoke in the distance. They stopped and stared.

"Reckon it's a town," Law said.

"We're going to stop, aren't we, John Thomas?" Sara Jane asked, her face suddenly brightening. They had passed a farm now and again, and each time she had asked if they could stop, but Law had always refused.

"Too dangerous," he explained the first time, and after

Sara Jane had complained, he added, "You know that Ellsworth has friends and kin all over the area."

He hesitated before answering now. He was wary, but he knew that the children, at least, needed a decent meal or two and a place to sleep other than huddled in blankets on the frozen ground. He also thought it might be a little safer in a town—at least a small one—than at an isolated farm. Or maybe he was tired, too, and just wanted to think that so he would have no excuse not to stop here. "Reckon we will," he finally said.

They moved on, their pace somewhat more brisk. As they rode, Law came up alongside Sara Jane. "Stopping here might cause us some difficulties, Sara Jane," he said.

"How so?"

"Those townsfolk'll most likely figure we're husband and wife."

"We'll just disabuse 'em of the notion," Sara Jane said primly.

"And then they'll know you're travelin' with a man who's not your husband, and they'll not look kindly on that, I expect, especially if this place is as small and out of the way as I figure it is. You know how such people like to wag their tongues."

"I don't much care what they think," Sara Jane snapped.

"Me neither," Law said. "But it might make it difficult for us to find a place to stay—if there's even a hotel or an inn here." He stared off into the distance, hesitant to look at her as he said, "But that means, like as not, sharing a room."

Sara Jane laughed, though it seemed a little forced. "I expect, if it's all that small a town, that we'll all have to share a room, in which case, my virtue will be safe." She blushed, thankful that he could not see it because of the scarf wrapped around her face.

Law looked back at her, and nodded. "I expect that if

anyone asks, we can make do I'm your new husband—that you were a widow when we wed recently." He refused to look at her, lest he see any pain in her eyes.

"I expect that'll be all right," Sara Jane said with a sigh. It seemed to her that the problems were never-ending these days. Even the smallest, most innocuous thing held danger of one sort or another. She was plumb tired of it all.

"You might want to instruct the young'uns," Law added quietly, "not to be too free in speaking about us to any townsfolk."

Sara Jane nodded. She didn't think it would be necessary, as she didn't think the children would be talking to anyone without her being right there.

Half an hour later, they rode into a small but neat town that a sign proclaimed to be Bakerville. There was only the main street, with a few buildings on each side: a saloon, a general store, some houses, a bakery, a dressmaker's with a law office on the second floor, a church, a tiny school, and a blacksmith shop and livery at the far end.

There was almost no one on the street, which was not surprising considering the weather, though Law saw people peeking out from behind curtains in some of the shops and homes.

CHAPTER 19

THE LITTLE GROUP stopped at the livery, which a sign proclaimed to be Ogilvie's. A short, burly man looked up from his forge just inside the partially open barn doors. He put the hot piece of iron and his hammer down. Wiping his hands on a piece of cloth, he came outside, apparently oblivious to the fact that he wore no coat or hat. The beads of sweat quickly disappeared.

"Afternoon, folks," the smith said pleasantly. "Name's Seth Ogilvie. Somethin' I can do for you?"

"Well, the horses and mules need tending," Law said. "And some grain, if you got it."

"I do."

"Is there someplace where we can stay the night?"

"Ain't no hotel or inn," the smith said. "But old Mrs. Harrington has an extra room and she'll take you in, like as not." He pointed. "Fourth house up there on the right. If you're of a mind to stay there, I'll have my son go up and tell her you'll be over directly."

Law glanced over at Sara Jane, who nodded gratefully.

"Obliged, mister," Law said. He dismounted and went over to take Walter from Sara Jane's arms. As he set the little boy down, he saw the blacksmith send a youngster of about ten years old running up the street. Law grabbed little Janie, lifted her down from her horse, and set her on her feet.

Ogilvie was already leading Toby into the barn. Law followed him inside. He had seen no evidence of it, but he wanted to make certain. "You have a telegraph office here in town, Mister Ogilvie?"

"Nope," the smith answered as he put Toby in a stall. "Town's too small."

Law paid the man the quite reasonable fee and explained how he wanted the animals cared for. He went back outside, picked up Walter, and began heading up the street.

As they walked, Sara Jane said, "I overheard you ask the smith if there was a telegraph in town. You hoping to wire someone?" She was considerably puzzled.

"Nope," Law said. "Just wanted to make sure no one here could wire someone."

"Like Ellsworth or the Pinkertons," Sara Jane said with sudden realization.

"That's right."

Moments later, they met Ogilvie's son, who was heading back to the livery. "Mrs. Harrington is waitin' on you folks," he said. "She said she'll have some supper cooked up directly."

Mrs. Harrington must have been standing with the door cracked because she opened it as Law, Sara Jane, and the children stepped onto the boardwalk. She was old and slightly stooped, with a shock of pure white, thinning hair. But her bright blue eyes and seemingly boundless energy belied her age. She wore a long, plain, black wool dress with a matching shawl wrapped around her shoulders.

"Welcome, welcome," she said. "Come in. Oh, you must be so cold, all of you." She closed the door and immediately began unbundling Janie.

Sara Jane began doing the same for Walter, as soon as Law put the boy down.

When they all were out of their winter garb and sitting around a long wooden table near the fireplace, Mrs. Harrington served Law, Sara Jane, and Lemuel coffee and the two younger children some tea. The aroma of sizzling sausage filled the room. Within minutes, Mrs. Harrington was serving up homemade sausages with gravy.

"Let me help," Sara Jane said, starting to rise.

"You sit, child," Mrs. Harrington said firmly. "You look near done in."

They all dug in hungrily, the fat-laced food filling and warming. Almost immediately after eating, Sara Jane put Janie and Walter to bed in the back bedroom they would all share that night. Lemuel stayed up with the adults for a short time, all sitting around the table, sipping coffee. Law lit a cigar and truly savored it for the first time in quite a while.

Still, it was not long before Lemuel, unable to keep his eyes open, retired, followed less than half an hour later by Sara Jane and Law. There were only two beds in the back bedroom. The two youngest children slept on one. Lemuel was wrapped in blankets on the floor against one wall. Law considered trying to talk Sara Jane into sharing the other bed with him, but decided against it. Asking such a thing of her at this time would degrade her, and he was not about to do that. Besides, as Mrs. Harrington had said, Sara Jane did look mostly done in.

Law grabbed a couple of blankets from the stack on a

chair and spread one out on the floor. Smiling wearily, Sara Jane only partially turned away from him as she rather brazenly removed the man's shirt and pants she had worn since helping Law escape and dropped them on the floor.

Law gulped seeing her in her cotton camisole and drawers.

Sara Jane offered him another grin, this one with a touch of sauciness. She bent and grabbed one of the pillows on the bed and playfully tossed it to him. With a giggle, she slipped into the bed.

Law caught the pillow and dropped it. Still with his eyes on Sara Jane, he took off his guns, setting them next to the blanket. As he stretched out, pulling another blanket around him, Sara Jane blew out the lantern. It was, Law thought, going to be difficult getting to sleep with those images of Sara Jane so fresh in his mind.

"CAN WE STAY here, Mister Law?" Lemuel asked the next morning after another delicious repast. He glanced around, making sure that Mrs. Harrington had not come out of her room.

"That would be nice, John Thomas," Sara Jane said.

"Maybe a day or two," Law allowed.

"Why not till spring?" Sara Jane asked.

"Still too close to St. Joe," Law said flatly. "And, I figure that every step we take toward Texas will be to our benefit. Besides, Sara Jane, there's nothing for me to do here. I couldn't just sit here on my hindquarters till the weather breaks."

Sara Jane was disappointed, but she quickly put on a brave face. She did not need the children seeing her downcast.

"Three days, then," Law said. "That'll give us time to regain our strength without wearing out our welcome with Mrs. Harrington."

"A week?" Sara Jane countered with a small smile.

"Four days," Law said with a sigh.

MRS. HARRINGTON REFUSED the money Law tried to offer her. "No, no, sir," she said. "It's been a right pleasure having company, especially children around me again."

"But I insist, ma'am," Law said.

"So do I, Mister Law," the old woman said. She had been told the story that Law and Sara Jane had concocted about him being Sara Jane's second husband.

"All right then, ma'am," Law said. "We're powerful obliged." He pulled on his coat.

"You ready, John Thomas?" Sara Jane asked, trying to keep the sadness out of her voice. She did not look forward to traveling again.

"Yep." He paused. "No, wait," he added. "I forgot something in the back room." He went into the room he and Sara Jane's family had shared. Making sure Mrs. Harrington had not followed him, he took a twenty-dollar bill and tucked it partially under the lantern on the small table next to the bed. He walked out of the room. "Let's go," he said. He grabbed Walter and swung him up onto his broad shoulders.

Law called out to Seth Ogilvie at the livery. The black-smith glanced out the door, nodded, then said something to someone deeper inside the barn. Moments later, Ogilvie and his son came out, the father leading a small farm wagon pulled by the two former pack mules, the boy with a saddled Toby and Sara Jane's sorrel unsaddled.

Sara Jane looked at Law in surprise.

"I gave Mister Ogilvie the pinto and the chestnut plus

some cash money for it," he said with a shrug. Seeing the look of surprise lingering on her face, he added, "I expect it'll be some slow going, but I reckon it'll be a sight more comfortable in many ways, especially for the two littlest ones."

"But who's going to handle the wagon?" she asked. "I've never done such a thing. I can handle a carriage, but I'm not so certain about . . ."

"Oh, hell, woman, you can handle anything you put your mind to," Law said gruffly. "But Mister Ogilvie's been teachin' Lem to drive it, so he can handle most of that chore."

Sara Jane looked at Law and smiled. "You are a most considerate man, John Thomas," she said. She still did not look forward to traveling in this frightful weather, but this would make it easier. Sitting on the hard wagon seat would be no fun, but at least she wouldn't have to ride all day, every day, holding Walter on the saddle in front of her.

They put Walter and Janie in the back of the wagon, the sides of which were two feet high, which would keep the children out of most of the wind. The children still had some room, despite the piles of supplies. There were several blankets and a couple of old buffalo robes to keep the children warm.

Law tied the extra horse to the back end of the wagon. He helped Sara Jane up onto the wagon seat after Lemuel had pulled himself up, then mounted Toby.

"Obliged for all your help, Mister Ogilvie," the bounty man said. He touched the brim of his hat. "All right, Lem, head on out."

The twelve-year-old, face set in prideful determination, slapped the reins on the mules' rumps, and the wagon clanked into motion.

They headed southwest, and four days later came to the

Vermillion River, which they followed, after a fashion—
preferring to travel in mostly a straight line rather than actually following all the curves and bends of the river—until
its confluence with the Kansas River. They debated riding
across that frozen river, until Law found tracks in the snow
over the ice a mile or so downstream. He decided it was
safe, and they made it across with no difficulty. Following
the instructions Ogilvie had given Law before leaving Bakerville, they turned more directly south, soon crossed the
Mill River, and continued on.

The traveling was rough as they fought the wind and
cold every step of the way. They got caught in a snowstorm
twice, which they rode out, huddled in a makeshift lean-to
Law and Lemuel had thrown together with a couple of
tarps Law had bought in Bakerville.

Almost two weeks after leaving Bakerville, they were
running low on supplies, and Law was wondering what to
do. The best he could figure from what Ogilvie had told
him, Topeka was maybe four or five days northeast. Law
did not want to backtrack, but more important, he didn't
want to go to a big place like that if he could avoid it. They
were still not all that far removed from St. Joseph, and he
figured the Pinkertons—and probably Ellsworth, if he had
gotten word of Law's escape and Sara Jane's having left
St. Joe—were still looking for them. And any arrivals at
this time of year would likely attract attention. It would not
take much for someone to hear about a "family" just entering the city in the dead of winter and investigate. He expected handbills had gone out with their descriptions. If
someone spotted them, it would be only minutes before a
wire was being sent to St. Joseph. A return wire might have
the local law come for them. If the Pinkertons wanted to
do it themselves, it would not be hard for determined
horsemen—or men who used trains where possible—to
quickly pick up their trail.

Late the next morning, they spotted a bit of smoke in the air. Law figured it was a farm, but he had to check it out. Settling Sara Jane and the children in a small copse of cottonwoods along the river, he rode ahead. On a rise, he pulled out his telescope and looked the place over. He was surprised to see that it was a trading post.

He trotted back to the copse and left Toby there with Sara Jane and the two younger children. With Lemuel beside him, Law drove the wagon to the trading post, bought some supplies, and headed out as quickly as possible. It disappointed the owner, who seemed to be lonely way out here pretty much by himself and wanted to gab, but that couldn't be helped. Law did not want to leave the Gibbonses alone any longer than necessary.

Law did talk with the man a little and managed to elicit the information that the city of Emporia was only a couple of days' ride south. So when they left the copse, Law headed them slightly southeast to avoid it. The day after the next, Law turned south again. If the information Ogilvie and the fellow at the trading post have given him was correct, he figured they should be miles from any larger city and would remain that way at least until they got to the Indian Nations.

Eight days later, they were running low on supplies again. Hoping to find someplace to restock, Law began riding out ahead of the others and soon came across a small town. He studied it for a little from a distance before deciding it would be all right to stop there, at least for a night. He had seen no telegraph poles and nothing else to indicate there was a lot of contact with other towns, at least at this time of the year.

Verdigris was slightly larger than Bakerville. It had one main street, with two cross streets. The livery was on the north end of town, from which Law's group approached. They passed it for now, riding into the town to look it over.

The mercantile store was bigger than the one in Bakerville, and there was a separate hardware store. The stage depot looked abandoned. There were fewer houses on the main street, though there appeared to be plenty on the side streets. A church was at the far end opposite a school, and there were two saloons, directly across the street from each other.

A door opened in an office and a man stepped out, stopping under the sign that said BARBER SHOP/DENTIST: Hot baths available. He was of medium height, with flamboyant chestnut-brown muttonchops that ran into a mustache. He wore a black overcoat and bowler, and spectacles were perched on his nose. "Howdy," the man said. "I'm Lloyd Rutherford, mayor of Verdigris. Welcome." He offered a mousy smile.

"How-do," Law said.

"We don't get many visitors this time of year," Rutherford said.

"We're just passing through, though considering the hour, we just might stay the night here. There some place we can bunk?"

"No hotel, but there's an empty house 'round the corner there on First Street you can use for the night for a small fee."

Law figured the mayor owned the place, but that didn't matter. As long as it was clean. "That'll do."

"I'll see to it a fire's lit right off, while you take the wagon and animals down to the livery," Rutherford said.

"Obliged. There someone who can cook up some grub for us? We're willing to pay, of course. Sara Jane here's got her hands full tendin' to the young'uns, and the trip has been wearing on her."

"That can be arranged. Leave it all to me." He did not move, though.

Law pulled out a five-dollar bill and leaned over a bit in the saddle to hand it to Rutherford. The mayor took it, nodded. "When you're done at the livery, turn here," he said, pointing. "Third house on the left. It should be open by the time you get back there." He turned and began walking swiftly up the street.

The house was, indeed, open when Law and the others arrived. It consisted of three rooms—two bedrooms at the back, and one large room that served as dining room, kitchen, and sitting room. A fire was blazing in the fireplace on the right-hand wall. There were several chairs in the sitting-room area. Forming a kitchen was a long, wood table, a cookstove, and several shelves that were mostly bare. A young, plain-looking woman with golden hair tied up into a bun was busy at the counter next to the cookstove. She smiled weakly. "Hope you don't mind fried salt pork and gravy," she said nervously. "It's fast and fillin'."

"That'll be fine," Sara Jane said. She would have eaten fried worms if someone else had prepared them for her.

"There's coffee there," she said, pointing to the pot on the table. "It's hot and purty fresh. I brung it from home."

AFTER EATING, LAW wandered over to the mercantile. A tall, spindly older man with thin hair and bifocals was waiting on a plump matron, so Law stood back a bit, to the side, waiting. Moments later, two young men burst in, boots thumping, voices loud. One wore a heavy, thigh-length canvas coat, a holstered six-gun belted around it, and a low, round-crowned hat; the other had on a full-length bearskin coat, a matching hat, and two pistols strapped around the outside of the coat.

The shopkeeper's face flashed worry, annoyance, and

fear. The woman patron said, "I'll be back, Claude," and waddled out as fast as she could.

The man in the canvas coat went behind the counter, shoving the shopkeeper roughly out of the way, and grabbed several sacks of tobacco from shelves behind the counter. He tossed two to his partner and stuffed the others inside his coat. He took some cigarette papers and added them to the stash in his coat, then took two pint bottles of whiskey from the shelves.

"Put this on our bill, old man," Short Coat said with a sneering laugh as he and his friend headed back out. If they saw Law back in the shadows, they did not acknowledge him.

When they were gone, Law asked, "That happen often?"

"All the time," the shopkeeper said. He was almost shaking. "'Least since those two come to town a couple months ago."

"Can't anyone stop 'em?"

"Who? Town ain't got no marshal. Them goddamn ruffians have the run of the whole damn town."

Law knew he shouldn't get involved, but he could not let the young men's arrogance and the fear it created in the old man go unchallenged. "Be back directly," he said and went out the door, unbuttoning his coat as he did. He saw the men heading up the street.

"Hey, boys!" he shouted. "Hold up there." When he got no response, he yelled, "Stop, you two pukes!"

The men halted and turned. "You talkin' to us, asshole?" Bear Coat said with a snarl.

"You owe the shopkeep some money, punks," Law said evenly.

"Old man Ahearn'll put it on our bill," Bear Coat said. "'Sides, it ain't none of your concern."

"I'm making it my concern, you chicken-livered scut.

Now either go on back there right now and pay up or . . ."

"Or what?" Short Coat snorted.

The two men laughed. The laughter stopped when Law shoved back the side of his coat, clearing his Peacemaker.

CHAPTER 20

LAW BEGAN WALKING slowly toward the two men. "So, what's it gonna be, boys?" he growled. "Shit or get off the pot." He did not care at the moment that townsfolk had begun watching—and listening.

Bear Coat sneered. "You ain't gonna do a damn thing, mister," he said, trying to snarl but not quite making it. "'Least you ain't gonna shoot us in the back." He and his friend started to turn, chuckling.

"You sure about that, you pinheads?" Law snapped. He drew his pistol and fired off a round, sending Bear Coat's hat sailing away. "Next one will be about six inches lower," Law warned.

The two turned, their condescension changed to anger and worry.

"That weren't very nice, mister," Bear Coat said. "That hat cost me a purty penny."

"You most likely stole it, bub," Law said, dropping the revolver back into the holster. "Now you can save the three of us a heap of trouble—and keep yourselves from getting killed—if you go and do what's right."

"Piss on you, goddammit," Bear Coat growled. He jerked out his pistol and fired off three shots in the blink of an eye.

Somewhere behind Law, a window broke. Where the other two bullets went he had no idea. By then, he had drawn the big Colt in his right hand and the smaller one in his left.

As Bear Coat let fly with three more shots and Short Coat unlimbered his pistol and cocked it, Law walked forward, firing, alternating shots from the two pistols—three from each.

Bear Coat fell first, his partner a second later. The former was dead when he hit the icy street, the latter twitched and groaned. Law approached Short Coat cautiously. He knelt and picked up the man's gun and pitched it away. "Goddamn fool," he muttered.

Short Coat just groaned again, then stiffened. His eyes opened wide, and his last breath puffed frostily out.

Law rose. With pistols still in hand just in case, he turned, surveying the area around him. No one presented a danger. People were venturing slowly out of their homes or businesses.

Mayor Rutherford hurried up. He looked down at the two bodies and grew pale. "That was some shootin', mister," he said, adjusting his glasses.

"And a mighty benefit to this town, too," the shopkeeper said as he came up and stopped next to Law and Rutherford.

There were murmurs of approval all around.

"You need me to write up something about what happened here, Mayor?" Law asked.

Rutherford looked at Law, then the shopkeeper, then Law again. "Reckon that won't be necessary. Claude here can tell me what brought this on. Considerin' all the deviltry these boys committed in Verdigris, it's good riddance to 'em both."

Law nodded. He looked at Claude. "I was wantin' some cigars," he said. "You got any?"

"Some," Claude said. "C'mon with me back to the store."

The shopkeeper insisted that Law take his entire supply of cigars—two dozen of them—free. Law accepted them and promised to return the next morning for supplies before he and Sara Jane left town. Then he went back to the house.

Walter was asleep by the fire. Sara Jane was in a rocking chair, back to the fire. Janie sat in front of the chair while her mother braided the girl's hair. Sara Jane had put on a dress; Law figured she had been embarrassed, dressed in men's clothing in the presence of their young cook. Lemuel sat at the table, eating a piece of pie.

Law poured himself some coffee and sat at the table with Lemuel. He lit up one of his new cigars. Lemuel grinned at him. "Miz Betsy makes some fine pie," he said.

"That so?" He glanced over at the young woman, who blushed.

"Yessir," Lemuel said with enthusiasm. "You ought to try some."

Law grinned a little. "Did you leave me any?" he josued. "The way you're eating, boy, I doubt there's a piece to be had in this whole town."

Lemuel looked horror-stricken, until he realized Law was teasing him. He laughed and went back to his pie.

"Would you like some, sir?" Betsy asked.

"Don't mind if I do." He stubbed the cigar gently out, saving it for later, as Betsy brought the pie. He was just finishing it when there was a knock on the door. His hand slowly lowered until it rested on the grip of his pistol as Betsy answered the knock.

Rutherford entered. "If I may have a moment of your time, sir?" he asked.

"Sit," Law said. "Betsy, please get Mister Rutherford some coffee."

"Obliged," the mayor said as he took a seat. He took a sip of coffee, then said, "I have a proposition to make to you, mister . . . mister . . . ?"

"Law," he responded, after a few moments' hesitation.

"That's funny."

"Since when is a man's name something to poke fun of?" Law demanded, though not very harshly.

"Not funny as in pokin' fun of," Rutherford said hastily. "Funny in an unusual way, considerin' why I'm here." He slurped more coffee, nervous. "The reason I come," Rutherford finally said, "is that . . . well, me and the other town officials have talked and we'd like to ask you to . . . well, we'd like to hire you as town marshal. I mean, after what you done today and . . ." He jolted back a little more coffee.

Law looked at the man as if he had lost all reason. Then he glanced at Sara Jane, who was staring at him with eyes full of expectation. "I'll need some time to think it over, Mayor," he said gruffly, feeling annoyance build inside of him.

"We'll pay you thirty dollars a month. No, fifty," Rutherford swiftly added.

"I'll let you know by morning at the latest," Law said. He quickly ushered Rutherford out.

He turned and smiled at Betsy. "I reckon it's nigh on time you got back to your family, Miz Betsy," he said gently. He wanted to talk this over with Sara Jane, and did not want an outside pair of ears listening in. "Would you like an escort home?"

"I don't think that's nec . . ."

"I'll do it," Lemuel burst out, leaping up.

Law managed to hide his bemused smile. "Is that all right with you, Miz Betsy?"

She smiled indulgently. "Yessir." She paused, then asked, "Do you want me here to make the morning meal?"

"Yes, ma'am."

As soon as the door had closed behind Betsy and Lemuel, Sara Jane said, "You are going to take the position, aren't you, John Thomas?"

"Lord, woman, give a fellah a minute to think on things," he said, more harshly than he had wanted. He sat back at the table and relit his cigar. He thought for a little while, then said, "I swore I'd never put on a badge, Sara Jane."

"Why not?"

"It just doesn't seem right, considering my history. Besides, I don't know as if it's a good thing to stay here."

"I know, we need to get back to Texas," Sara Jane said, sounding a bit exasperated. "But the children are suffering something awful, John Thomas." She didn't much care about herself. She would survive, no matter how hard it got and no matter how unused to this kind of life she was. But she worried fiercely about her children.

"Supposin' someone found out we were here."

"That's not likely. There's no wire here, as you noticed right off. And no stage service this time of year. We're miles from anyplace with trains or telegraphs. I was talking to Betsy while you were gone. She says the nearest city is Emporia, and that's at least three days' ride from here. Wichita's maybe a week, and Kansas City some more than that."

She could see cracks in Law's resistance. "We can wait out the winter in safety here, John Thomas," she pressed. "Safe from the elements, and, I think, reasonably safe from discovery. When spring comes, we can move much faster, and without the danger of freezing to death."

Everything Sara Jane had said was reasonable, but Law was still reluctant.

"And, unlike when we considered staying in Bakerville, you'd have something to do here. Something important."

Law stewed over it for a minute or two, then realized it made sense. The Pinkertons would never think of looking in such an out-of-the-way place for them. And, while Ellsworth might have some kinfolk in the area, the chances of it were slim. As best he could tell, Ellsworth was a Missourian, and it was likely that his relatives were mostly in that state or perhaps south.

"All right, Sara Jane," he finally said.

THE JOB WAS not difficult, as there was very little crime in Verdigris without the two men Law had killed. And as time passed, Law began to relax somewhat, though he never dropped his alertness. He and Sara Jane were accepted into the small community, though they were careful to keep to the lie about their relationship in public. Sara Jane quickly found it easy to respond to being called Mrs. Law. She wondered about that some days when she was alone, thrilled at the notion at times, at others feeling as if she were betraying Oliver. She had to admit to herself, though, that she did not think about him very much these days, and that increased her guilt. But with the children to care for, she could often push it out of her mind.

At Sara Jane's suggestion—and with Lemuel's enthusiastic backing—they hired Betsy to do the cooking for them, leaving Sara Jane to keep up the house and take care of the children.

Law kept to himself mostly. He found no one in Verdigris with whom he could get too friendly. There was no one of Abe Covington's or Billy Tyler's character or caliber. Still, he would spend a little time in the saloons of an evening, if only to keep away from the house for a while.

Being there in such proximity to Sara Jane and not being able to touch her was difficult, more difficult than anything he had come up against in a long time. Though they shared a room to keep up their pretense, he slept on the floor.

As the weeks passed, they settled into something resembling normalcy. Sara Jane was glad to have a home again, even one as small and lacking in amenities as this one, and help around the house. She enjoyed caring for the children, and she found that Betsy was more like a sister in many ways than just a hired cook and sometime maid. Both doted on Janie and Walter, and the two children reveled in the attention. Lemuel had turned thirteen a couple of weeks after they had arrived in Verdigris, and had let it be known that he no longer needed nearly as much of his mother's attention as the younger children. When he was not staring rather moon-eyed at Betsy, he spent time with Law. He liked the big, hard-eyed man, who treated him more like a young man than his father had.

For his part, Law did not mind having Lemuel around. The boy was full of questions many times, but he actually listened to the answers, which was more than Law could say about many grown men. And with Verdigris being the peaceable place it was, Law did not mind taking Lemuel with him on his rounds or to his office—a small place next to the Verdigris Saloon that had once been used by a lawyer, until the attorney had decided there was not enough business in Verdigris to keep himself in beans and had left. Mayor Rutherford had seen to it that he had a desk and a chair and enough wood for the small stove. Law had provided himself a coffeepot, which he kept going on the stove most of the day, and a few tin mugs.

The one thing Law did not show Lemuel was how to use a gun, though the youngster often asked. Law did not think it wise, and Sara Jane adamantly opposed the idea. When Lemuel was pestering Law about it again one day,

Law said, "We've been over this a passel of times before, Lem. You're too young just yet."

"But, John Thomas . . ." He had started calling Law John Thomas, with Law's permission.

"No, Lem," Law said flatly. Wanting to assuage the boy's disappointment, he added, "What say we go on over to Claude's and get you some penny candy?"

Lemuel's eyes lit up.

They headed to the store, waving to Sara Jane and Betsy—and the two younger children—who were entering the small milliner's/seamstress shop a few doors up from Ahearn's mercantile.

"Now, you make sure you get some of that candy for your brother and sister, Lem," Law said with mock severity when they entered Ahearn's. "No more than twenty-five cents' worth, though." Law greeted Ahearn and asked for coffee and sugar. He spotted some cookies that Mrs. Ahearn had baked up fresh that morning and took some of them, too. He figured it would be nice to have something to nibble on with his coffee when he was alone in the office.

Lemuel finally had picked out his candy and brought it to the counter, where Ahearn wrapped everything in paper. Law paid him and indicated with a nod that Lemuel should carry the packages.

With candy to be had, and figuring he would even get a cookie or two, the boy didn't mind. He grabbed the packages and headed for the door. Law opened it, let Lemuel through, then stepped outside himself.

And all hell broke out as two men on horseback let loose a hail of bullets.

CHAPTER 21

LEMUEL FELL WITH a yelp and a moan, packages flying. A window shattered. Sound and bluish gunsmoke filled the cold air.

"Sons a bitches!" Law bellowed. He saw Lemuel going down out of the corner of his eye as he instinctually went into action. He slid a few steps to his right, jerking out his big Peacemaker. Another window broke with a crash behind him. A woman screamed somewhere nearby.

Law considered fanning his pistol—which he always thought an inefficient and foolish way of firing the Colt—to lay down as heavy fire as he could in the quickest time, but decided against it. He fired fast but evenly, coldly thumbing back the hammer and squeezing the trigger as rapidly as he could. Bullets thudded into the wall behind him and one tore splinters out of the hitching post in front of him.

He hit the man nearest him at least twice with his first three shots, his face exploding in blood and bone. He fell when his horse reared, the animal catching a bullet from

Law's pistol in the chest as it did so. It fell next to the man, squealing in pain and trying frantically to get back to its feet.

Law swung the pistol to the left and kept firing. The gunman grimaced as a lead bullet punched his right shoulder back, and he dropped his pistol. He wheeled his horse and spurred it hard, racing up the street.

Law kept firing, but the pistol was out of ammunition. He dropped it into the holster, tore open his greatcoat, and reached for the smaller revolver in his shoulder holster. As he stepped into the street, a screaming woman rushed past behind him. He was vaguely aware that it was Sara Jane, who knelt next to Lemuel and cradled his head in her arms as she continued screaming, tears coursing down her face.

Law thumbed back the hammer on the Colt, ready to fire, but the wounded gunman was too far away for a safe or accurate shot. He glanced at Lemuel and Sara Jane. The boy, who had been trying to show he didn't have to listen to his mother, had left his coat unbuttoned. His shirt was soaked in blood.

Rage burst through Law like a locomotive plowing through a slight snow drift. He jammed the revolver back into the shoulder holster and ran, coattails flapping, as if a grizzly were on his heels. He stormed into the barn at the livery, passing its wondering and surprised owner. In minutes he had Toby saddled and bridled. Then Law swung into the saddle and kicked the horse into motion.

The big buckskin, sensing his master's urgency, tore out of the barn. Law tugged the reins, and Toby almost went down as he turned, his hooves slipping and skittering on the snowy ground. But he righted himself and raced on.

Law flattened himself somewhat along the horse's neck, yelling encouragement and slapping the ends of the reins of the buckskin's rump. The big horse surged forth long legs reaching, stretching, hooves pounding. His head bobbed rhythmically, and the great chest pumped as he hit a ground-covering stride.

Despite the racing pace, Law could see spots of blood here and there as he galloped past. But a couple of miles outside of town, he stopped seeing them. "Goddamn!" he roared into the rushing wind. He brought Toby to a slow halt, then turned the blowing animal and rode slowly along his back trail, eyes searching the ground, trying to keep his anger in check, knowing that if he didn't, he would never pick up the track again.

Then he spotted it. The rider had turned off onto a small trail toward the northwest. "Let's go, boy," Law growled, pushing Toby into a run again. They raced along. A mile or so on, they topped a very low rise and tore down it, Law pulling the horse to the right a bit to go around a small stand of cottonwoods along a creek. Then he spotted the farmhouse. He jerked Toby's reins hard, and the horse almost went down again as its hooves slid.

Law pulled the buckskin around and trotted back to the trees. He stopped and dismounted. He swiftly reloaded the big Colt, then took out his telescope and surveyed the farmhouse perhaps a quarter of a mile away. He counted five men saddling horses in a small corral to the left of the house. He continued to watch. As he did, his mind played over what had happened. He realized that he recognized—or was fairly certain he did—the men in town. The one he had killed was Dan Fouquette, and the other was Charlie Quinlan—both of whom had escaped from jail with Ellsworth. He guessed that the men saddling horses down there included Ellsworth.

His rage boiled over again. He wanted nothing more than to just ride on down there and blaze away. But a kernel of common sense remained, preventing him from doing that. For one thing, he wasn't sure if these, indeed, were Ellsworth's men. It's possible the man he had been following had turned off again, and this was a perfectly innocent bunch of men. He didn't believe it, but it was possible. More important, he didn't know if there were more men inside the farmhouse, and worse, if they might be holding an innocent family hostage.

So he waited, letting the fury inside him simmer. The image of Lemuel lying there cradled in his mother's arms, his chest covered in blood, kept the rage fresh and powerful.

He watched as the men mounted up and began galloping toward him. He continued watching through the telescope. As they got within several hundred yards, he could begin to make out features. He was glad that Marshal Fairburn had shown him the photographs that had been taken of Ellsworth and his men during their trial. Soon he was certain of all but one, whom he assumed was the occupant of the farmhouse. The only question was whether he was a willing participant.

Law rose, eyes hooded with hate and rage. He took a box of cartridges from a coat pocket and filled the empty bullet loops on his gunbelt. He put the box of shells back into his pocket, then took off his coat and tossed it on a bare bush. He pulled himself into the saddle. "Time to make those bastards pay for what they done to Lem, old boy," he said to the horse, patting him on the neck.

With that, he rode out of the barren trees and onto the trail. There he stopped and waited, his ire keeping him warm in the cold air.

The five horsemen stopped when they saw him, then continued on their way. They stopped again when they were about a hundred feet from Law. "Looks like you done saved us a heap of ridin'," Ellsworth, who was in the center, said almost jovially. He was a bull-necked, bull-bodied man who strained the canvas coat he wore with two guns strapped outside it.

Law glared at his opponents—Matt Keekins, who had a

face like someone had smashed it flat with a frying pan; Bart Ragsdale, a medium-sized man with the look of a moron about him; Charlie Quinlan, whose features were etched in pain and whose wool coat was covered in blood high on the left side of his chest; and the man Law didn't know, a big, doughy-looking fellow with cautious eyes. Now that he saw the man up close, Law remembered seeing him in town not long ago, though he did not know him and had seen him only the once.

"You and these other pukes got a lot to answer for, Ellsworth," Law finally said.

"The hell you say," Ellsworth allowed. With the odds highly in his favor, he was in fairly good humor. "It's you who's got a heap to answer for. You killed five good men."

"They were scum, just like you." Law paused. "How'd you find me, anyway?"

"Cousin Elmer there," Ellsworth said, nodding toward the man Law did not know. "He knew I was lookin' for you, you son of a bitch, and when he went to town and saw you, well he got himself up to Emporia and wired me in . . . well, where it was I was."

Law turned icy eyes in Elmer's direction. "That was a goddamn fool thing to do, bub." He swung his gaze back to Ellsworth. "I usually give even assholes like you a chance to give up and try to make things right." He loosely looped the reins around the saddle horn and pulled his Peacemakers, one in each hand. "But not this time." He kicked Toby's sides with his heels and bellowed a rebel yell as the horse bolted ahead.

Ellsworth and Meekins, just to his right, reacted first, spurring their horses forward as they drew their pistols. They split as they rode, moving at an angle to come up on Law from each side, so as not to allow him easy targets.

Law had expected it, and, figuring that Ellsworth was the more dangerous, gently prodded Toby toward the outlaw leader with his knee. But even as he did, he let loose two shots in Meekins's direction. Meekins fell, and his horse trotted on again before slowing, stopping, then returning to where the outlaw lay.

Sitting tall in the saddle, even as Ellsworth shot at him, Law kept bearing down on the outlaw leader. He fired twice, from little more than twenty feet away. One bullet tore into Ellsworth's side, and the other into the side of his head. The outlaw leader was punched from his horse and landed with a bounce on the hard ground.

Knowing he had killed the man, and not needing to see him hit the snow and ice, Law veered slightly to his left and kept racing forward. Bart Ragsdale had just gotten his pistol out and fired off a round or two. Law returned the fire. Bullets slammed into Ragsdale, who reeled in the saddle, back arched awkwardly. His horse dashed off, the outlaw flopping wildly on its back.

Toby kept running, heading straight for Elmer, who sat on his horse, frozen with fear. The buckskin veered of its own accord at the last second. Elmer's horse reared in fright, dumping its rider on the ground. Elmer's head hit the ground, stunning him a bit.

A few yards on, Law slowed Toby and then stopped, turning the horse. He shoved the smaller Colt away and swiftly reloaded the bigger one, watching Quinlan.

The man had followed Meekins forward only moments after the latter had charged. When Meekins had been knocked from his horse by Law's bullets, Quinlan had stopped. He wondered whether he should flee. His shoulder wound was still bleeding, and the pain was intense. Then he had seen Law blast Ellsworth, then Ragsdale, and send Elmer flying. When he saw Law reloading, he figured he had only this one chance, and he had to take it. If he didn't, he knew Law was going to follow him no matter where he ran. He spurred his horse toward Law.

The bounty man watched, calmly reloading, the rage still burning white hot inside him. He wanted to kill them all, but none more so than Charlie Quinlan. It was Quinlan—even though it might have been Fouquette's bullets that were actually responsible—who had put Lemuel down.

Law snapped the loading gate of the Colt shut and brought the pistol up. He rested the barrel across his left forearm to steady his aim. Beginning when the wildly firing Quinlan was fifty feet away, Law emptied his revolver at the man, who was drilled off his horse, which kept running.

Keeping watch over the now silent battlefield, Law reloaded the pistol again, then edged Toby forward. He stopped alongside Quinlan, whose face was unrecognizable after three of Law's bullets had ripped through it. He rode on, checking on Meekins, who was dead, then headed for Ellsworth.

The outlaw leader was still alive, though in bad shape. Law dismounted and loomed over Ellsworth. The rage that had burned in his chest threatened to erupt again.

Ellsworth, who was lying half on his side, was trying to cock his pistol.

"You murderous sack of shit," Law hissed, the fury bursting forth. He brought up a booted foot and smashed it down on Ellsworth's gun arm, snapping it in two places. The outlaw leader howled, but Law was unmoved. "You goddamn evil bastard," Law said as he began to stomp and kick Ellsworth's face, head, chest, and stomach. He was beside himself with rage, unaware for some minutes that Ellsworth had died under the assault.

Finally he came to his senses and looked down without a shred of remorse at the battered corpse. He turned and mounted Toby, then rode to where Elmer was just getting to his feet. The farmer's face was white with fear.

Law dismounted and stared at the man for a few moments as the fury that had consumed him faded to the dull ache of loss. He didn't know what he would do without Lemuel tagging along with him anymore. He pulled the Colt, ready to kill the man who had brought all this destruction. Then he stopped himself. He stepped forward and slammed a fist into Elmer's face, knocking him on his ass. "I ought to kill you, you verminous shit pile," Law growled. "But I won't. Not just yet, anyway. Now get up." When Elmer had done so, Law grabbed the old pistol out of the belt around Elmer's coat. He emptied it and tossed it as far as he could. Then he said, "Take your horse and walk. That way." He pointed to where Ellsworth's horse was standing near its master's body. He followed on foot, towing Toby behind him.

"Stop," Law ordered when they were still a few feet away. He went to the horse and pulled out the Winchester from the saddle scabbard. Handing Ellsworth's horse's reins to Elmer, Law smashed the rifle on the ground. He gathered up the outlaw leader's pistols, emptied them, then peeled off the dead man's holsters. He stuck the pistols in them, then hung the gunbelt over his own saddle horn.

"Get his body up on the horse and tie it down," Law commanded. As Elmer started doing so, Law got pistols and gunbelts from Meekins's and Quinlan's bodies and put them with Ellsworth's on his saddle horn. Meekins's horse was the only other one around, and Law got the rifle from it and broke it. He went back to where Elmer was struggling to get Ellsworth's body on a skittish horse that refused to stand still.

"When you finish that," Law said tightly, "get Meekins's body on his horse. I'll be back directly."

"Where you going?" Elmer asked, a fleeting burst of hope blossoming in his breast.

"Find Quinlan's horse and Ragsdale's." He glared at Elmer. "You leave here, or you try anything stupid, and I will stomp you to death just like I did your clap-ridden cousin."

He was back much more quickly than he had expected. Elmer had finished his work and was sitting forlornly on his horse, looking wistfully toward his home. Ragsdale's body was still on his horse, so there was no work to be done there. While Elmer was getting Quinlan's corpse on his horse, Law rode to the trees and retrieved his coat. Then Law had Elmer lead the way back to Verdigris, towing four corpse-laden horses.

Just about the entire town turned out to watch the odd little procession ride in. Law stopped in front of Mayor Rutherford's barbershop/dentist office. Rutherford nodded when he saw Law.

The bounty man did not bother to dismount. "Lock this wretched puke up somewhere," he said, chucking a thumb at Elmer. "I don't give a good goddamn what you do with the bodies." He turned Toby and headed down Main Street, then turned onto First Street. He dismounted and tied Toby off—vowing to get the animal proper food and care shortly. With a heavy heart, he entered the house.

CHAPTER 22

"JOHN THOMAS!" SARA Jane shouted, leaping up from her chair.

"Sara Jane," Law said. He had never felt so helpless, so inadequate. How could he ever apologize for being responsible for what happened to her oldest son? But something seemed strange about her, and in a moment it hit him. She did not seem particularly devastated.

Before Law could say anything more, a faint voice came from one of the back bedrooms, "That you, John Thomas?"

Law's eyes widened as he stared at Sara Jane.

The woman nodded, face beaming through tears of joy. She came up to him. "Lem's alive," she said. "He's bad hurt, but he's alive."

Law shoved past her and entered the bedroom. Lemuel lay on the bed. He was whiter than the snow drifts, but he smiled bravely, though wanly. His upper right chest was swathed in bandages. Law could only stare in wonder.

"Mayor Rutherford's something of a doctor as well as a

dentist," Sara Jane said from right behind Law. "Between him and Betsy, they got Lem patched up pretty good. The bullet went clean through."

"How're you feelin', boy?" Law asked gruffly, moving close to the bed.

Lemuel wanted to cry, it hurt so much, but he was not about to let Law see that. "It's paining me some, John Thomas," he said, through gritted teeth. "But it's not so bad, I reckon."

"Oh, pshaw," his mother said. She smiled at her son, then looked up at Law. "He's been asleep most of the time you were gone. And it's time he was asleep again," she added firmly, her gaze going back to Lemuel.

"But, Ma . . ."

"No arguing, son," Sara Jane said firmly but lovingly. She took the bottle of laudanum and a spoon from the table next to the bed. She gave him a dose, which the boy did not fight.

Lemuel snuggled deep into the covers. He looked up at Law, his eyes already growing heavy. "Did you get the skunks who did this?" he asked.

Law nodded gravely. "I sure did, Lem. The two who actually did it, and the others who sent 'em here."

"That's good." Lemuel closed his eyes.

They went back into the main room. Janie and Walter were quietly playing near the fire. Betsy McCallister was working at the stove. She looked over her shoulder. "Are you hungry, Mister Law?" she asked. "I've got some sausage and gravy cooked up."

"That'd be good, Betsy, thank you," Law said as he sat at the table. He was still having trouble realizing that Lemuel was alive.

Sara Jane sat across from him. She reached out and rested her small hands on his big, callused ones. "Was it bad?" she asked.

Law shrugged. "Not so bad," he allowed. "The two who

kill . . . shot Lem were Ellsworth's men. I tracked the one who ran to a farmhouse a few miles from town." He nodded thanks as Betsy put mugs of coffee in front of him and Sara Jane. Law took a sip and almost managed a smile. Betsy had dosed it with a healthy dollop of whiskey. "Ellsworth and what was left of his gang were there. They were getting ready to come here after me. I disabused 'em of that notion," he finished flatly.

Betsy put a plate, knife, and fork down before him, then a platter of biscuits.

"How'd they learn you—we—were here?"

Law took a bite of food, thinking for the thousandth time that Betsy was a damn good cook. Between mouthfuls, Law explained, then said, "I told Mayor Rutherford to lock Elmer up till I decide what to do with him."

"Elmer?" Betsy asked. "Elmer Doherty?"

Law shrugged as he continued to eat. He had realized two bites in that he was powerful hungry. "Never got his last name. Big, dumb cuss looks like he's made out of bread dough."

"That'd be him," Betsy said.

"You know him?"

"Sure. Not well, mind you. But we townsfolk get to know all the farmers hereabouts, at least a little. He never seemed a bad sort."

"Maybe he ain't, but he's a goddamn fool . . ."

"John Thomas!" Sara Jane scolded.

Law just glared balefully at her. "He's a damned fool," he went on, with the barest teasing smile at Sara Jane, "for getting mixed up with that scum. And he might be good at heart, but by tellin' his cousin I was here, he almost got Lem killed."

"What are you going to do with him?" Sara Jane asked.

"I ain't certain. He's lucky I didn't kill him along with the others." He finished eating, then had Betsy pour him some more coffee. He lit a cigar. Then he sighed. "I reckon Elmer ain't like the others, but I'm not of a humor to just let him go. Because of him, a young boy nearly died, and five men are dead. That can't be easily excused."

He sat there smoking his cigar a while, thinking. Something had been bouncing around in his head since he had started riding back to town, and it was only now beginning to coalesce. "But Elmer's not going to be our problem for long," he suddenly said.

"Oh?" Sara Jane countered, surprised.

"It's time we left Verdigris, Sara Jane," Law said. He ignored the quickly quashed gasp from Betsy.

Sara Jane looked at the girl. "Would you please go check on Lem, Betsy," she said. "Just make sure he's all right."

"Yes'm," Betsy said, disappointment spreading over her face.

"All right, John Thomas," Sara Jane asked when Betsy had left, "why do we have to leave Verdigris?"

"For one thing, I reckon the good people of Verdigris might be powerful worried that I'm going to keep attracting trouble."

Sara Jane looked dubious.

"But the main reason is that if Ellsworth found us, the Pinkertons just might do so, too."

"But Ellsworth had a cousin tell him where we were," Sara Jane protested.

"True. And it's not likely that someone is going to go running to the Pinkertons and tell them where we are. But the Pinkertons—and a heap of other lawmen—have been looking for Ellsworth. With the reward on him and his boys, there's a mighty good chance somebody will get word to the Pinkertons if they saw Ellsworth in the vicinity. Or even heading this way."

Sara Jane's shoulders sagged. He was right, and she knew it. And it wasn't as if she had any great love for this town.

But she had grown fairly comfortable here and, even though she knew they would be leaving in several weeks anyway, she didn't like the feeling of being on the run. But she nodded. "When?"

"Soon as possible."

"What about Lem?" Her heart sank as she thought of her seriously wounded son. "Moving him could be . . . could . . ." She could not bring herself to say it.

"He's a strong boy, and he'll survive," Law said. Seeing the pain on Sara Jane's face, he added, "We'll coddle him as much as we can."

"And I'll help," Betsy said. She had come up behind Sara Jane and gently laid her hand on the woman's shoulder.

Sara Jane looked up at her, surprise on her face again. "You don't know what you're saying, girl," Sara Jane said, not at all unkindly.

"Yes, I do," Betsy insisted. "I've come to admire you and Mister Law a powerful lot, and I've come to love the children."

"What would your parents say?" Sara Jane interjected.

Betsy shrugged. "They might miss me some, I expect, but I got my own life to live." She suddenly looked close to tears. "I'm fifteen and ought to be gettin' married soon, but there ain't many prospects here in Verdigris. Just some foolish young boys, and old man Lyman's been showin' an interest." She almost shuddered at the thought.

Sara Jane looked at Law, who shrugged and said, "It's your choice, Sara Jane. I got no objections, and I expect she'd be a mighty big help to you along the way." His thoughts were already elsewhere.

Sara Jane rose and faced Betsy with a smile. "I reckon the children'd favor having you along. I would, too. If you can talk your folks into it, we'd be right proud to have you come with us."

Betsy's face lit up.

Sara Jane grew serious. "But you might want to cogitate on this," she said. "We have a long, long way to go, it's not spring yet, and we have to get through some bad country, I expect, on the way. It won't be an easy trip, Betsy."

"That's all right," the girl said, still beaming. "I'm gonna go talk to my folks right now." She grabbed her coat and bonnet and hurried out.

TWO DAYS LATER, just after first light, Law gently lay Lemuel in the bed of the wagon and covered him with a buffalo robe. It was still mighty cold, though Law thought he could feel a hint that spring was coming. With the help of Lloyd Rutherford and Claude Ahearn, Law piled some supplies in after the boy, then lifted Janie and Walter into the wagon bed. While Law helped Sara Jane up onto the wagon seat, the mayor did the same for Betsy. Law tied the extra horse to the back of the wagon.

Law went around and shook hands with Ahearn, then Rutherford.

"We're sorry to see you folks go," Rutherford said, sounding pretty much as if he meant it.

Law nodded. He smiled and pulled the badge off his coat and handed it to Rutherford. "Elmer's your responsibility now, Mayor," he said, with something that approached a smile. They had already talked this over, and Law had decided to let Rutherford make the decision on what to do with Elmer Doherty, who had been kept chained in the abandoned stage office. Law had visited Doherty the afternoon before and warned him that if Rutherford let him go he had best keep his mouth shut about Law. "You saw what I did to Ellsworth and his boys," Law had said flatly. "I get wind that you've sent anyone after me, I will not hesitate to hunt you down and kill you in the most painful way I can think of. If the mayor lets you go, I'd suggest you head on home to your family and forget you ever even heard of me."

Doherty, images of Law stomping Ellsworth to death playing in his head, had gulped and nodded.

"Well, you have a safe journey now," Rutherford said.

Law nodded again and pulled himself into the saddle. He touched the brim of his hat at Rutherford and, in general, the small crowd that had gathered to see him and the others off. "Let's go, Sara Jane," he said.

The woman clicked her tongue and slapped the reins on the mules' backs, getting the wagon into motion. With Law riding to the left side of the wagon, they headed south down Main Street. A mile or so outside of Verdigris, Law swung them west.

Startled, Sara Jane looked at him. "West?" she inquired.

Law nodded. He had given it considerable thought. Lemuel's condition was serious, and a journey of a couple of months, including a long stretch through the lawless Indian Nations, would be mighty tough on the recovering boy. "We'll catch the train at Wichita," he said.

Sara Jane's eyes widened further. "What about the P . . ."

"I reckon we can take the chance," Law said flatly. "They've got no reason to look for us there." He did not know how much, if anything, Sara Jane had told Betsy about their troubles with the Pinkertons, but he didn't want to mention them until he knew for sure.

Sara Jane was worried, but relieved at the same time. Even with the time it took to get to Wichita, taking a train would cut their journey from two months or more to two weeks, maybe even a bit less.

Law kept them riding long hours, and early on the fifth day after leaving Verdigris, they were on the edge of Wichita. Law stopped them. Leaving them there in a small stand of ragged, stunted trees along a slim strip of a creek, he rode into Wichita by himself. There, he checked on when the train would be leaving next and bought tickets. Then he rode back to where the women and children were.

By then he was aware that Betsy knew much about their plight with the Pinkertons and so felt free to speak in front of her.

"Train leaves just after noon tomorrow," he' said, after tending to Toby and sitting by the small fire, getting some coffee. "We'll stay the night here." Seeing Sara Jane's questioning look, he added, "Spending even one night in a hotel might give someone a chance to talk."

He took the dish of beans Betsy handed him and spooned some down. "If the Pinkertons are there, or even have eyes there," he said, "they'll be looking for a man, woman, and three young'uns. And unless it's some of them we've had dealings with before, they likely won't know what we look like. So what I figure to do is have you two ladies and the children go into town on your own and get on the train. With Betsy along, that might throw anyone off, since they won't be looking for two women, a wounded young man, and two children. I'll be nearby, close enough to keep watch over you, but not to be seen with you. I'll get on the train a bit after you."

"What about the wagon and mules?" Sara Jane asked. "And the sorrel?" She liked that horse.

"Just leave 'em somewhere near the depot. Take only your personal bags and leave everything else." He hated to do it, seeing as how it was a waste of money, but it couldn't be helped. The less contact they had with anyone in town for any reason, the better.

"That's cruel to the animals," Sara Jane protested. "I don't care about the wagon, but the animals . . ."

"Somebody'll steal 'em," Law said flatly, certain he was right. "At most they'll be there overnight before some enterprising cuss makes off with 'em."

The next day, Law had them wait until past midmorning.

"I don't want you getting there too early," he said. "If you have to stay round the depot for any time, it increases the chances that you'll be seen—if anyone is looking. I doubt that, but we need to be cautious."

Law rode alongside them, but just before they reached the outer fringes of Wichita, he loped ahead. He had something to do, and he wanted to take a look around the area before the others arrived. The check showed him no one who appeared to be a Pinkerton, and he felt reasonably good about it. Then he went to the telegraph office. He had debated doing this since he had decided to come to Wichita, and was still not certain it was the wisest thing, but he felt it safe enough. Long ago, he had learned that Marshal Fairburn trusted the telegraph operators in St. Joe, and Law figured Wichita was big enough that if the Pinkertons were around, they would not have been able to bribe all the operators here. At the office, he handed the operator two messages he had written out, and waited until they were sent. The operator did not seem at all suspicious or anxious. Law got his originals back and paid the man.

He hurried back to the depot, where he stayed in the shadows of a nearby building, and watched as Sara Jane and the others arrived. She stopped at the depot. Law was irked, until he realized she was just hiring a boy to help her with the bags. She moved on and parked the wagon in an isolated spot. Within minutes, helping Lemuel walk, she, Betsy, and the children were on the train, which wasn't scheduled to leave for another twenty minutes.

Law got Toby into the livestock car, then hung around until the last minute. He saw nothing suspicious, and he swung himself up into one of the cars just before the last call for boarding.

CHAPTER 23

THE WELCOMING COMMITTEE in Austin was small but full of smiles. The happiest was Walter Godfrey Woodall, who rushed to Sara Jane and wrapped her in his arms. Both father and daughter wept, but after a few moments, Sara Jane pushed Woodall away and introduced her children.

"Where's Mama?" Sara Jane asked, after Woodall had greeted the children.

"She took sick," the mutton-chopped man said. Seeing the alarm on his daughter's face, he quickly added, "It's just a touch of grippe. She'll be fine soon."

Abe Covington and Billy Tyler greeted Law warmly, though Tyler's gaze swiftly turned to Betsy McCallister, much to Lemuel's annoyance.

"We thought you was done for, J.T.," Covington said.

"Damn near came to pass a couple of times, Abe," Law said with a grin. He had not said much in his wire from Wichita—only that he was heading back to Austin with Sara Jane and that it would be good if the Ranger captain could make sure there were no Pinkertons at the train station when

Law's group arrived. The other telegram he had sent was to Marshal Fairburn to request the reward on Ellsworth and the others.

"Who's the young lady?" Tyler asked, eyes still on Betsy.

"Betsy McCallister," Law said. He saw the look on Tyler's face. "Sara Jane hired her on to cook for us in Verdigris, up in Kansas, where we stayed a spell." He smiled a little. "But you best be careful 'round that one, boy," he joshed. "Lem there's got his heart set on her."

Tyler nodded, not really paying attention. He was so smitten he could not even come up with one of his humorous and odd rejoinders.

"I take it Lem's one of Sara Jane's young'uns?" Covington said, shaking his head at his subordinate.

"The oldest," Law answered with a nod. "He took a bullet meant for me, which is why he looks a mite peaked."

"You'll have to tell me all about it."

Law nodded absently as he watched Woodall ordering several people to gather Sara Jane's things and help the children into buggies.

"And now's a good time as any, J.T.," Covington said. He knew Law was annoyed at Woodall hustling the woman off right away.

Law shook off the feeling of gloom. It was as if he were seeing Sara Jane for the last time, though he knew that was not true. "Reckon a good meal and a few beer's be in order," he said.

Over a large, seared beefsteak, beans, and yams at Mickleson's, Law told the two Rangers what had transpired since Tyler had left St. Joseph.

"No wonder you didn't want no Pinkertons in your welcomin' party here," Covington said when it was told. "I ain't seen any in some weeks, though. There was a passel of them assholes here not long after Billy got back, about, I figure, the time you . . . ah, left . . . St. Joe. In fact, they was bein' such a pain in Billy's ass that I had to send him out on patrol against some Mexican bandits. I knew them Pinkertons'd never follow him on such a venture. They finally all left after a spell, figurin', I suppose, that you weren't comin' back. Hell, we all figured you'd up and went under out in the wild somewhere."

They ate a little more, then Covington said, "The reward money on those boys you snuffed in Verdigris is waitin' at the bank."

Law nodded thanks.

Covington hesitated, then asked, "You ever heard anything more about Sara Jane's husband?"

"Nope," Law responded flatly. He still didn't like talking about the man, and had managed not to think about him in some time. "I have no idea if he's been snuffed out or lit out for parts unknown." That got him thinking about Sara Jane again, and he started getting annoyed. He hadn't even really had a chance to talk to her for a moment before her father had whisked her away.

Covington knew instinctively what Law was thinking. "They're stayin' at the Manor House tonight," he said.

Law managed a small smile. "That obvious about my affections for her, was I?"

Covington nodded, but there was no derision in it. "I made sure the place had a room for you."

"Obliged."

"So what're you sittin' here for?" Covington said with a grin.

Law nodded and rose. Slapping on his hat, he grabbed his coat—which he didn't need here—and stalked out. A few minutes later, he had dropped his greatcoat in his room. Before pulling on a frock coat, he looked at himself in the mirror. His once-white shirt was filthy and his vest a bit frayed. He took a moment to run some soap and water over his heavily stubbled face, and he ran a hand through his hair. "Hell with it all," he muttered. He marched out of the room and knocked on the door to Sara Jane's room.

Woodall answered. He seemed as if he were about to refuse Law admittance, until he saw the look in the bounty man's eyes. He stepped back and opened the door.

"Howdy, John Thomas!" Lemuel said cheerily. He still looked rather pasty but was recovering nicely.

"Howdy, Lem," Law allowed, grinning a little, He shifted his gaze. "You all right, Sara Jane?" he asked.

"I am." She looked tired but happy. "Papa and I were just talking about where I'm to live for the time being." Her face became defiant and determined. "We finally agreed that I'll be staying in Austin, at least for a spell."

Law did not show his relief.

"He thought the children and I would be safer out at the ranch with him and Mama, but I think we'd be safer here. The Pinkertons 're not likely to try something here in the city, with you and Captain Covington and others about."

"I agree," Law said.

"But she will not be staying here, in the Manor House," Woodall added from behind Law.

Law could understand that. "I aim to come callin'," he said, aiming his words at both Sara Jane and her father.

"That would not be proper," Woodall said, moving up and around to face Law, though not quite between the bounty man and Sara Jane. "She is a married woman."

Law glared balefully at him. "If Mister Gibbons shows up, I'll defer to him," Law said. He would honor that statement should it become necessary, but he hoped it would not. "But we don't even know if he's alive."

"That does not matter," Woodall said. "It'd not be proper."

"You mind if I come calling, Sara Jane?" Law asked.

"No, John Thomas," she replied, ignoring the angry look her father threw in her direction. "I don't mind at all."

* * *

IT WAS SOMETHING of a strange existence for Law and
Sara Jane. They had lived under the same roof for a considerable time, though had done nothing that could be
deemed improper. Law courted her now in Austin, but both
were uncertain, so proceeded slowly. Much of the uneasi-
ness between them was because they didn't know if Gibbons was alive or dead. With that specter hanging over
them, and Woodall's frequent presence, they were cautious
around each other.

Despite his courting of Sara Jane, Law got itchy after a
couple of weeks. He was not a man to sit around doing
nothing. So when he heard about a pair of outlaws—with a
reward of fifteen hundred dollars on each—who had wandered deep into Texas from their usual haunts in the Indian
Nations, Law decided to go after them. It took only a few
days to track them down, and he finally crept up on their
small camp on Yegua Creek northeast of Austin.

Law pulled back a ways and tended to Toby. He cat-
napped through the night, and just before dawn, he edged
up on the camp again, tying Toby to a bush twenty yards
back. As pinkish-gray light began tingeing the east, Law,
who was behind a live oak tree that was beginning to leaf,
called out, "Rise and shine, boys! It's time you paid for
your devilish ways."

The two rolled out of their blankets, pistols in hand.
Law did not hesitate, just opened fire, making short work
of the two. He reloaded his Colt and walked into the
camp. Making sure both were dead, he went and got
Toby. He decided not to bother saddling the outlaws'
horses. He got some rope from one of their saddles and
cut off a few lengths. Then he tossed one body over a
horse's back and tied it down, and did the same with the
second. He poured himself some coffee from the outlaws'

fire. He was drinking it when a snapping twig caught his attention. Slipping out a revolver, he faded into the brush to the side.

He moved through the trees, heading toward where he had heard the sound. He stopped every few seconds to listen, each infrequent sound helping him zero in on whoever it was out there. He finally spotted someone creeping up on the camp, and he eased up silently on the man. He suddenly jammed the muzzle of his Colt against the back of the man's head. "Howdy, bub," he said.

The man raised his hands. "Don't get nervous with that piece, mister," the man said nervously.

"Who are you?"

"Name's George Underhill. I'm a Pinkerton detective. I've been trailing these fellows for more than two weeks now."

"Looks like you're a bit late, bub."

"You a bounty man?"

"I am. And I took these pukes down fair and square, and I aim to claim the reward on 'em."

"Don't seem fair to me, not after all the trailin' I've done."

Law pulled the pistol away, uncocked it, and dropped it into the holster. "That's your tough luck, bub." He took a step back and one to his right.

Underhill suddenly whirled, ready to attack Law, who simply smashed him on the side of the face with a fist. Underhill went down. Law knelt over him. "You are one goddamn dumb bastard, mister Pinkerton detective," he said. Law took the man's holstered pistol and the derringer he found after patting him down. He stuck both guns into his pocket, then grabbed Underhill's shirtfront and hauled him to his feet.

"Best ride on, bub," Law said. "And don't cross my path again." He spun and walked to Underhill's horse, grabbed

the Winchester rifle from the saddle scabbard, then the outlaws' rifles, and jammed all of them under one of the bodies. He swung up onto Toby and rode slowly off.

Law was wary on the trip back to Austin, alert to the
possibility that Underhill might try to attack him some
night. But the ride was uneventful, and the next day, Law
pocketed his three thousand dollars. He escorted Sara Jane
to dinner that evening, much to Woodall's annoyance. But
Sara Jane discounted her father's worries, reminding him
that few people in the bustling big city of Austin knew of
her situation.

They began to relax a little more with each other, especially as Lemuel began really recovering, which helped set
Sara Jane's mind at ease. Law and Sara Jane enjoyed each
other's company, though they often wondered where this
relationship was going. There were no answers, however.

Law finally broached the possibility of Billy Tyler
courting Betsy McCallister to Sara Jane. She had known
how Lemuel felt about Betsy, but in the past few days, her
son had begun to attract the attention of several girls his
own age and was showing less interest in Betsy. Because of
that, Sara Jane gave her assent to Tyler courting Betsy,
though she left the decision up to the young woman. Betsy
gladly agreed that it would be a good thing.

A week after Law had returned with the two dead outlaws, he headed over to Covington's office to tell Tyler the
good news. He was almost there when he was stopped by a
booming voice: "John Thomas Law!"

He turned slowly, his good spirits turning surly when
he saw seven Pinkertons lined up against him. Among
them were Milt Dalrymple, Ned Rogers, William Iverson,
and George Underhill, who still sported a colorful bruise
on his face. All were dressed in town coats, buttoned only
at the top; four wore bowlers, two derbies, and the other a
Stetson.

Traffic on the street came to a halt as riders and wagon drivers cleared out of the way. People scurried for cover.

"You have a long list of crimes to answer for, Law," Dalrymple said. He was again in his element—the center of attention. "Not the least of them is bank robbery, escape, and attacking two Pinkerton detectives."

"Those charges are either old or bogus, and you damn well know it, Dalrymple," Law said. He unbuttoned his frock coat, tugged it off, and dropped it on the ground.

"Like hell," Dalrymple said. He was enjoying himself and thought the people would be behind him, since he had listed Law's crimes. "You are under arrest, Mister Law. Now submit and allow us to take you back to Missouri, where you'll have a fair trial and then be hanged."

"I don't reckon that's going to happen," big Abe Covington growled, as he moved up alongside Law on the bounty man's right.

"This is our jurisdiction," Tyler said, stopping just to Law's left, "and you got no more business bein' here than a donkey does at a church social."

"Anywhere we want to go is our jurisdiction," Dalrymple snapped, not at all pleased with this turn of events.

"Not in Texas, asshole," Covington said. "Now we got papers from two judges in Missouri and one here in Austin that dismiss any charges you may have brought against Mister Law. So I suggest you get back on the next train and haul your asses out of Texas."

"Everybody knows Texans're nothing but goddamn liars," Dalrymple snarled. "We're taking Law back to Missouri one way or the other." He eased his pistol out, and everyone else on both sides began doing the same. "And killin' a few goddamn Texans to do so won't put us out none. Now stand back or . . ."

"Then make your play, boy," Covington said flatly.

Law saw the Pinkerton on the end to his left raise his

pistol, and he whirled and snapped off a shot at the man. Gunfire erupted, and within seconds, clouds of gun smoke clogged the air. Law swung back toward the center and fired off three rounds at Dalrymple, feeling a bit of satisfaction when all three bullets punched holes in the Pinkerton.

As he swung toward another target, Law saw Rogers driven back by several bullets, his back hitting a hitching post, where he hung by one arm for a moment before crumpling to the ground. He fired off the last two rounds in the Colt, thinking he had hit another Pinkerton, but he could not be sure because the gun smoke was too thick.

Then Law felt a bullet tear into the side of his abdomen, just under the bottom rib. He grunted with the impact and the pain, but kept his feet. He shoved the big Colt away and yanked out the smaller one. Another bullet creased his upper left shoulder.

"Hold your fire!" someone bellowed. "Hold your fire!"

The shooting faded to a stop. Law crouched, waiting warily. He glanced to his right and saw Covington still standing, using a wagon for protection, and seemingly unhurt. To Law's left and slightly behind, Tyler was resting against a post holding up the portico in front of the Ranger office. He had a small, bloody line on his shirtsleeve over the bicep.

The smoke cleared, and Law spotted two of the Pinkertons hiding behind barrels of nails in front of the hardware store across the street. One rose, holding his pistol up and sideways, showing he was not ready to fire it. "There's been enough killing here today," he said. "I'm Phil Stratten. Now that Matt Dalrymple's dead, I'm the ranking Pinkerton detective here, and I say this fight is over."

"What about J.T.?" Covington asked.

"You swear on your badge that when you said you had papers exonerating him from a couple of judges that it was the whole truth?" Stratten countered.

"Every word."

"Reckon that's the end of it, then." He put his pistol away. "The rest of my men, put up your weapons."

The other Pinkerton behind a barrel rose and slid his weapon away, and Iverson came from around the corner of a building, also holstering his weapon. The three moved toward their fallen comrades, two of whom, including Underhill, were down, but alive.

Wary, Law holstered his Colt, but stayed where he was. The thought of getting up from the crouch was not too exciting at the moment. Covington and Tyler came up, got Law to his feet, and began helping him down the street, heading for the doctor's.

Sara Jane suddenly charged up and shoved Tyler out of the way. She slipped Law's left arm over her shoulders. "You best not die on me, John Thomas Law," she scolded, tears in her eyes. "You just best not."